DATE DUE	

m

The

First, there were the "accidents" — except Nate Tibbetts was certain there was nothing accidental about them. Only his quick-wittedness had saved his life on at least three occasions.

Mingled

Second, there were the unbearable, almost paralyzing headaches, followed by prolonged blackouts. And he began to wake up in unfamiliar places.

Seed

Third, there were the visions — his uncanny ability to know something was about to happen before it occurred — and strange thoughts inside his head that surely weren't his own.

Somehow, these were all connected, Nate knew, and he had to find out how…

…if he wanted to go on living!

Also by Neal Proud Deer

fiction

Trickle, Trickle, Fountain Flow
The Timechange Imperative
Survival of the Fittest
Mindtrapped!
Christmas Lost: A Fable
(with Martin Pope)
Hold Your Nose for America
& Other Stories
Cures, Crimes & Catastrophes
(coming soon)
Janus Warning (in progress)

non-fiction

Lights...Camera...Arch!
(with Foreword by John Goodman)
Selling's Magic Words
The Black Press & the Search for Identity
Blacks and the Press
Race and the Times
Shalt Thou Kill?
The Centrality of Peace in Baha'ism
War and Thought

The

Mingled

Seed

Neal Proud Deer

To the Readers
of Ozark Regional Library
— Read, read, read...
wordclay *and enjoy life!*

Neal

The Mingled Seed
By Neal Proud Deer
Lokman Edition Copyright © 1982
Neal Proud Deer
Revised Version Copyright © 2008
Neal Proud Deer

First published by Wordclay on 12/23/2008.

ISBN: *978-1-6048-1412-5 (sc)*

Wordclay
1663 Liberty Drive, Suite 200
Bloomington, IN 47403
www.Wordclay.com

Printed in the United States of America on acid-free paper.

To Ruth Anne,
my sweetheart,
my treasure,
my wife

"Thou shalt not sow thy field with mingled seed."

— Leviticus 19:19

PROLOGUE

Cancer!

He couldn't believe it. He didn't want to believe it. They couldn't make him believe it.

But it was true. He knew it was true. She really had cancer.

Why her? She had never done anything to deserve this. She was always a proponent of the "clean life." No drinking, no smoking, not even any swearing. To church every Sunday. But what had it gotten her? Cancer, that's what!

It wasn't fair. Here she was just barely over 40, and yet she was dying. Mama was dying.

Oh, God, if you're up there — I know I haven't been talking to you much lately, but please hear me now. Please. Pleeeeze, don't let her die. Do something. Anything. Just don't let her die. Please, God.

No use. Too late. Too late, the doctors had said. It had spread too far. Now, it was inoperable. A matter of weeks only, maybe even just days. And then he'd be alone. His father had been killed in that first war with Iraq. There was no memory of him. He'd been just too young. His brother Otis dead of pneumonia when he was ten. And now, Mama. He would be the last.

Funny, really, when he thought about it. Those experiments she'd told him about. The ones she and Daddy had taken part in before he was born. Cancer experiments. Cancer *cure* experiments. And now she was dying of cancer. Ironic. No, ridiculous. No, sickening!

Nathan Tibbetts struggled into the hospital's waiting-room toilet just before the sledge hammer inside his head sent him reeling.

Counter Operations Nullification and Tactical Reconnaissance Observation and Logistics (CONTROL) force: Created under classified action by Congress as part of the National Security Act Amendments of 1955 and empowered to seek out and eliminate, through clandestine operations, internal threats to the security of the United States of America.

CHAPTER ONE

"Beautiful, isn't it?"

Nate glanced up and stared at her luscious brown face. He was aware that Casta had spoken, though he had not the slightest inkling what she had said. But that seemed to make little difference to her. She went right on talking.

"So peaceful and quiet. I could just stay here forever, drinking it all in."

She focused on his eyes, and Nate nodded.

A crooked smile made its way onto her lips. "It's a good thing I ain't gonna give you a quiz on what I just said," she added, finally.

"I'm sorry, Cass, I..." He saw Babes coming, and he shifted his gaze toward the other, thankful that he didn't have to complete that thought. He knew what was behind it, but he didn't really feel like vocalizing it.

"Are you guys ever gonna hit the water?" Babes asked, pulling himself up onto the rock where Nate and Casta were seated. He looked directly at Nate, his sea-blue eyes penetrating, it almost seemed, into Nate's soul.

Nate shook his head. Babes shifted his gaze to Casta. "What about it?"

"Why not?" she responded. "I'm going in, even if you aren't, Nate."

She stood, and the sun glistened on gorgeous her

skin for an instant. Then she took Babes' pale hand and jumped into the water. "Br-r-r-r," she screamed. "It's like ice."

"You'll get used to it soon enough," Babes said, leading her out into the deeper water. He looked back toward Nate. "Sure you won't join us?"

Nate stood, but he did not move toward the water. Instead, he stepped away from the others, once again taking in his surroundings. Yes, it was peaceful here. A cool mountain stream surrounded by sheer rock cliffs on both sides. Water so clear its depth might be deceiving. Gurgling over rocks. School work left behind. With just the five of them. Martin and Shirl were somewhere near downstream. He couldn't see them, but he could hear them laughing and splashing.

It was too gorgeous, and he knew he shouldn't be here — not today.

Finally, he dropped his five-foot-eleven, light brown body back onto the rock where he had been sitting beside Casta, seconds before. He tried to think, but he couldn't. The birds wouldn't let him. Chirping, chirping, always chirping. Spring used to be his favorite season, but not any more. Not ever again.

The loud splashing drew his attention, and he looked up. But instead of seeing Martin Yeager and Shirley Wynn swimming back up stream, he saw Otis.

"Now, don't y'all go out in the deep part, ya hear me?" Mama was saying. "And stay together. You 'member 'bout th' buddy system."

She sat on the bank watching them splash around.

Actually, there wasn't any deep part here. Nate knew that, and he knew that Mama knew it, too. But she just couldn't resist an opportunity to caution them.

Mama was dressed in a mini-skirt, her legs tightly squeezed together and turned sideways on a blanket that she had brought along. A cardboard box filled with goodies set beside her.

"Told y'all you'd like this place. Your daddy usta bring me here when we was goin' together." But it had taken all this time, more than a decade, for her to get over him enough to bring them here, too.

"Yeah, Mama, can we come here a lots?" Otis asked.

"Now, I don't know about a lots, Brother, but we'll come back again. Y'all 'bout ready to eat?"

"Yea-ah," Nate shouted, passing his younger brother as the two of them raced to get out of the water. "What'd you bring, Mama?"

"You just get ya'self dried off, then we'll see what's in here." She nodded toward the cardboard box and grinned. "Just like your Daddy — always thankin' 'bout food."

She had started pulling things out of the box — chicken, potato salad, black-eyed peas — and was spreading them around the blanket when they heard the first clap of thunder. Seconds, later, Nate felt the first of the gigantic rain globules splash against his skin.

"Uh-oh, we better git to the car fast, boys," Mama shouted, scooping up the food and shoving it back into the box.

They sat in that old '78 Chevy for nearly an hour, watching the rain come down in torrents. Finally, when it slacked up, Mama cranked the car and drove away. They ate the food later, at home, and they never — ever — returned there. Less than a month later Otis died of pneumonia, and Nate knew it was the memories that kept her from bringing him back: memories of a husband and a son both having fun at that place and now both dead.

"Hey, you ready to eat yet, man," Nate heard someone say. He tried to focus. Finally, he could see that it was Yeager. Martin was grinning broadly. "You haven't even got yourself wet, have you?"

"No, not yet," Nate replied.

"Hey, don't worry about it. You're probably the only sensible one in the crowd. That water's as cold as a witch's tit. But I betcha Carmichael's been hassling you, right?"

Nate nodded, trying to smile. After all, Martin was simply trying to be friendly.

"Well, don't let that jerk give you any grief."

"Who you callin' a jerk?" Nate could see Babes climbing out of the water behind Martin.

Yeager whirled. "You — that's who. After all, it was your idea to come here, wasn't it?"

But Nate could tell they were both kidding.

"I'm about ready to dig into the grub, that's all," Yeager added, finally.

"Yeah, me too." It was Cass, climbing out onto the rock behind Carmichael. Shirl was still splashing around.

"Hey, fish, you want to come out and eat?" Martin was now asking Shirl, but she didn't bother to respond. He looked around at the others.

"Do we have to put this thing to a vote or something?"

"I'd say just go ahead whenever you're ready. We got chips and dip and weinies and stuff like that," Babes said. "Just eat whatever you want whenever you want it. Me, I'm going back in for a few more minutes first."

Carmichael jumped back into the water and swam toward Shirley. The other two came over and sat down on the rocks near Nate.

"How was it?" he asked, as Casta snuggled her soggy body next to his.

"Cold." She squeezed her head down into her body and drew her knees up toward her chest.

"Sure is!" Martin echoed.

"But it's nice. You should go in; really, you should,"

she added.

"She just wants to freeze your butt, too, that's all," Martin offered. "After all, this stream's an equal opportunity freezer. Right, Cassie?"

Casta grinned at the red-haired, freckled Yeager. "Sure," she said, squeezing Nate's left arm tightly with both her hands. But he knew what she was telling him — that he should get his mind off it.

As they ate, Nate studied Casta's features for perhaps the millionth time. Her beautiful milk-chocolate complexion, high cheekbones, and generous lips had sent his heart racing since first setting eyes on her. His own lighter skin and narrow nose, along with his green eyes belied his African ancestry. Especially the eyes had caused him much grief growing up. The other kids called him all kinds of names. He didn't really understand it. There weren't any Caucasians in the recent history of his family, and his mother was definitely not the type to "mess around." He guessed it was just "slave-owner blood" showing up after all those decades. Still, Nate wondered, especially since his brother had displayed the more typical African-American features....

He watched as Casta dipped one of the chips into a can labeled "Mexican style bean dip," then hustled the chip toward his lips. Yes, he was definitely lucky to have a woman like Casta Jordan.

"Um-m-m. I like that," he offered.

"Good. I can see your taste buds still work, Tib, but I'm afraid if you want any more, you're going to have to get it yourself."

He laughed. "Come on, now, Cass. You wouldn't let a man starve, would you?"

"I don't see nothin' wrong with your hands."

He laughed again, and this time he meant it. He also decided he'd definitely test the water later on. She winked at him, and he felt a stirring below. That was, after all, the thing that had captivated him first. He'd been eating a burger in the cafeteria and trying to get into Tolstoy when he first became conscious of her. When he looked up, he realized that she was staring. And she didn't drop her gaze for fully a minute. Then, just before she looked back down at the food in front of her, she winked. It was the most powerful wink he had ever seen in his life. It almost knocked him out of his chair. That had been almost a year ago. Less than a week after that meeting, they moved in together. He was already in love with her by then, and it didn't take him long to realize that he wanted to spend the rest of his life with this woman. Their wedding was planned for June, right after he graduated.

Out of the corners of his eyes, Nate could see that Shirley and Babes were climbing out of the water, and he turned his attention to them. He really hadn't been very fair to Babes, he decided, whom, he suspected, had organized this whole excursion specifically for his benefit — to try and cheer him up. After all, Carmichael had been the first white friend he'd cultivated on campus three years ago upon arrival. And they should be departing Wehling U. at the same time also, both graduating a year early next month. Carmichael was a little older than most undergraduates — in his late 20's or early 30's, though Nate didn't know exactly what. He'd never asked, and the other had never volunteered his age. Nevertheless, Nate had perceived Carmichael's sensitivity about his age and had given him his nickname. Strangely enough it stuck. Up until then, he'd simply been Larry, but now he was "Babes" to practically everyone on campus.

"Why haven't you brought me here before? Why wait till we're nearly through with school?" he asked, as the other strolled toward him.

"Didn't discover this place myself until last month. What do you think? Then, again, you haven't been in yet, so any assessment you make, at this point, has to be premature. Right, Yeager?"

Martin nodded. "Probably. It's definitely got the coldest water this side of Alaska."

Nate stood. "Listen, you guys trying to talk me out of going in for some reason? Trying to keep it all to yourself?"

Babes grinned. "I'll let you be the judge of that after you take a dip."

"Well, don't think I'm not going to," he shouted as he ran across the boulder on which he had been sitting, stripping off his shirt. A second later he was standing in water almost up to his strad. He was certain icicles were dangling from his knees.

"Where the hell does this water come from, anyway," he chattered, as he moved out into the deeper part.

"I've got a feeling that it definitely doesn't come from hell," Babes said, smiling. "Say, didn't they ever teach you not to go in right after eating?"

"Sure, sure. But I can tell you I'm not going to be in here long enough for the water to do me any damage." With that, he dove head first into the current, remembering that he never warmed up until he got his head wet and moved around some. He swam several strokes under water, trying to keep his eyes open to examine the other inhabitants of the stream. However, his effort didn't continue long. He had never been able to do that. Otis used to kid him about it. And he'd tried, endlessly, when they would go swimming, but, no matter what, the instant he went under, his eyelids would snap shut. It was as though they were controlled by a trap door activated by water. Finally, he'd given up trying after Otis' death. It just no longer seemed important to him. As he came up for air, he wondered why he had tried it today, after all these years.

Someone was shouting something at him, but his ears were too filled with water, and, for some reason, it didn't seem important enough for him to stay and listen. So, under again, he went, still trying. For Otis, he told himself, urging his eyelids, again and again, to open. He'd been under far too long, he realized suddenly. His body felt like it was about to explode, but he wouldn't let himself come up. Not yet. Concentrate. Just a little longer. Try! He had to keep trying. Finally, he could see light filtering in at the fringes of his eyelids. Then, more. Suddenly, he found himself staring at a large speckled fish not more than five feet away. At last, the pressure on his lungs made him give up the effort and move toward the surface.

As he felt the air go gushing out of him and the new air flooding inward, he was also filled with a deep satisfaction.

"Christ! Don't ever do that again!" he could hear Yeager shouting. "You were under too damn long."

He could feel the splashing, and he looked around to see a red head moving toward him. The other stopped a few feet away and began to tread water.

"Don't you ever do anything in moderation?" Martin asked. "First, you refuse to go in. Then, you eat and immediately jump in and stay under water forever. Christ! You gave me a scare."

Nate could see the other members of his party staring at him from the top of the boulder.

"I'm okay, now. I just had to prove a point — to myself. I'm getting out now." He began to swim back toward the others.

Babes extended a hand and helped him climb back onto the gray rock. Yeager was right behind him.

"You alright?" Carmichael asked in a subdued voice.

"Sure. I'm fine," Nate said, nodding. Casta slipped an

arm around his waist, and he kissed her lightly on the lips. He saw that all eyes were focused on him.

"Look," he added. "I can take care of myself. I've been messing around in the water since before I can remember. My brother Otis and I used to — well, we went swimming a lot, that's all."

Babes slapped him on the back. "Great. But I'm ready to head back unless you or somebody else wants to hang around a while. I don't think I want to go back in that refrigerator." Babes nodded toward the stream.

"I'm ready," Nate said.

"'Course getting back out of here ain't gonna be the easy job it was getting down," Babes added. Nate remembered the tedious chore of coming down on ropes, and he heard the factitiousness in Carmichael's remarks. He had wondered then, and it occurred to him again now, that there must be an easier way to get to this spot — by swimming downstream, or something. But he kept his thoughts to himself.

Martin, who claimed to have a good deal of experience climbing cliffs, went first. Next was Shirley, then Babes, Casta, and Nate brought up the rear. They paused several times during the next fifteen minutes to catch their breath. Numerous ledges along the rock wall further broke into their stress.

Sweat droplets formed at the base of Nate's hairline and rolled down his cheek, dripping off his chin. The rope encircling his body just below his armpits felt tight and uncomfortable.

And he had a bruise on his right shin from a slipped footing a few feet below. Nevertheless, his concentration was focused elsewhere. Again.

Then his attention was suddenly drawn back to reality.

A loose stone under his left foot was traveling, rolling away from the rock surface and taking his foot with it.

He tried to find a secure toehold with the right foot quickly, but there was none. The tips of his fingers were arched into a rigid grip on the rock surface, though he could feel them slipping, too. A lump in his throat chose this particular moment to make its presence known, and he could feel the thunderous beating of his heart, as if it were pounding at the walls of his chest, attempting to escape the confines of his body.

Abruptly, the rock under his left foot was gone, and his foot was dangling. The searching right foot slipped away also, and he felt himself plunge downward. But only a short distance. There was a sudden jerk as the rope caught, leaving him hanging about five feet from a ledge he had paused at only seconds before. He reached out with his right foot, trying to touch the ledge, but it was still more than two feet away.

He heard a scream from above him, and he realized it was Casta.

"Hold on!" A male voice, a few seconds later. He recognized it immediately as Babes'. "I'm on my way, Nathan. Just don't move around too much. And don't look down. Got that?"

Nate glanced downward immediately. God! He hadn't realized they had climbed that far already.

"Yeah, I, uh, got it, uh, Babes. I'm alri — "

But he wasn't alright. He felt the rope begin to inch him further downward.

Now, he looked up, and he saw the cause. A few feet above his head the rope was more than half severed and seemed to be unraveling. In the fleeting seconds that he hung there, staring upward, he could feel himself slip ever-so-slightly downward even more.

"I'm coming. I'll be there soon, Nate. Just hold still, now. Whatever you do, don't move!"

More advise from above. But this time, Nate knew he would have to ignore Babes' counsel. The rope just couldn't hold him much longer.

Rocking his body, he began to sway back and forth. He found that he could swing within a foot of the ledge. But, at the same time, he could feel the rope slipping more.

"Goddammit, Nate, stop that!" he heard Babes shout just above him. "The damn rope's unraveling."

But Nate continued to sway. Now, he could touch the ledge with his foot, but he couldn't make it quite far enough to get the foot onto the rock surface. More slippage. The rope couldn't hold out much longer, he knew. He had to make it next time.

He shoved his foot against the ledge and threw himself much further outward. Now, he was swinging back and —

Snap! But his feet landed securely, and he grabbed onto the stub of a dead bush which had tried to survive on the rocky surface. The bush hadn't made it, but it had helped Nate preserve his life.

Clinging to the dead bush, breathing rapidly, he felt the end of the severed rope dangling down beside him.

A moment later, a hand touched his back.

"He's safe!" Babes shouted up to the others.

INTERLUDE A

"*He has some loyal college friends, I gather.*"
"*Yes, but, besides the girl, only one is close.*"
"*Yes, I see what you mean.*"
"*The others shouldn't pose a problem.*"
"*No. I should think not — at least, not for one of your caliber, Panther. You have a contingency plan, I presume.*"
"*Yes, sir, I have a couple in mind. One is simple and direct. The other would require a little preparation.*"
"*And both would appear accidental?*"
"*They could be made to look that way.*"
"*Excellent. We can't afford to take any chances.*"

CHAPTER TWO

"The state of the art — if it can still be seriously called such — has been in decline for almost three thousand years." Professor Sidney Alland uncrossed his legs and threw his body off the desktop and began his almost ritualistic stroll around the classroom. When he had reached the rear, he whirled his stringy, six-foot, two-inch frame and began stroking his graying goatee.

"Consider Homer's *Iliad*, the epic masterpiece of all time. Yet it was written in the Ninth Century B.C. I ask you: What is *that* elusive quality of literary genius that evades modern writing? Can mankind ever recapture his lost heritage? I say, 'Nay!'"

Alland's eyes shot around the room, at last focusing on a pudgy, blonde youth in its center.

"Mr. Butler!" the teacher shouted.

The youth's eyes shifted toward Alland, but Nate suspected the other was avoiding focusing on those eyes. "Yessir?" he said, at last.

"Mr. Butler, do you think any modern writer has the potential of being read three millennia hence?"

"Well, I — "

"Indeed, if any modern writer's material will even exist three thousand years from now?"

"Uh — "

"Can you name one contemporary writer whose material can seriously be considered 'classic'?"

"Perhaps — "

"*No!* You cannot! Nor can any of you — for there are no great writers alive today. There have been no great writers in the last century. Why do you suppose that is" — Alland's gaze shifted again — "Ms. Halvorsen?"

Pompous bastard. Who set him up as the final authority on world literature? Nate really didn't care to listen to any more of this nonsense. He glanced down at his watch. Thank God class was almost over. And thank God he would be graduating in less than a month and leave Alland and all his kind behind.

Graduation. Oh, yes, he would soon hold his college degree in hand. That had once seemed like a glorious achievement. But not any more.

The end-of-class bell was sounding, and he began to gather his things together.

"Tomorrow, we will begin discussion of Virgil and his somewhat-less-dramatic contribution to Western literature," Alland was saying. "And Mr. Tibbetts, could I see you a moment before you depart?"

Nate glanced up. What? Why did Alland want to talk with him?

His books under his arms, he strolled down to the front of the classroom. Practically everyone else had left by now, and Nate found the room almost quiet enough to enable him to think. He stood silently, facing Alland, waiting for the instructor to speak. Alland was still watching the others depart. When the two of them were alone, he turned his attention to Nate.

"I understand you will be graduating in June, Mr. Tibbetts?"

"Yes, sir, that's right."

"You have plans?"

"Sir?"

"For after graduation? Career plans? Will you be continuing your academic career?"

"I'm not certain, Dr. Alland."

"Oh, I see. I had supposed an ambitious young man like you would have his entire career mapped out by now. I understand you have completed your education in three years instead of the customary four."

"Yes, sir, that's correct."

"Nothing unusual about that. Often, our students chose to go continuously — without summer breaks. Only you didn't do that, did you?"

"No, sir." What was Alland getting at?

"You have finished in three years by taking heavy loads each semester; am I right?"

"Yes, you are."

"And you're only 19? You finished high school when you were 16?"

"Seventeen. I was 17. I'm almost 20 now. My birthday's week-after-next."

"Oh, I see."

"Sir. I have to — "

"I'm taking up too much of your valuable time, right? And you want to know what all this is about? Why the 'third-degree,' as they say?"

Nate nodded.

"Very simple, my young friend."

Alland reached into his coat pocket and pulled out an envelope and handed it over to Nate. Nate held the envelope in his right hand, staring absently at it.

"Go ahead. You may open it," Alland prompted.

Nate pulled out two tickets.

"They're for Jonah's," the professor continued. "For tomorrow night. Afraid I cannot attend. It's a revival of *Our American Cousin*. Have you ever been to Jonah's?"

Nate shook his head. "No, sir."

"It's a dinner theater, and these tickets cover only the performance. I'm afraid you'll have to purchase your own meal. I hope you enjoy yourself."

Nate slipped the tickets back inside the envelope and stared into Alland's dark-brown eyes. "Oh, but I do have one question."

Alland nodded. "Why you, right?"

"Yes."

"Very simple: Since I had these tickets, I didn't want them to go to waste. And besides, I'm thinking of starting a new tradition. I may award tickets each semester to my best student. Kind of a bonus. Satisfied?"

"Yes, sir."

"Good." Alland slapped Nate on the left shoulder and began to pick up his notes off the desktop.

Nate began to stroll away. At the doorway to the classroom, he paused and looked back toward Alland.

"Thank you, sir."

Alland looked up and smiled. Nate was certain that was the first time he had ever seen him do that.

On the walk to his apartment at the campus' edge, he removed the tickets from the envelope three times to examine them. *Our American Cousin*, he remembered, was the play that Lincoln had been watching when he was shot. Did Alland really consider him to be the best student in that class or had he given him these tickets simply because he was African American and might appreciate the historical significance of the revival of this drama? No, that seemed to be stretching the elastic of credibility a bit too much. But Alland had never shown any interest in him before.

Why now? Oh, what did it matter? And, anyway, he hadn't made up his mind if he would attend. After all, he would have to pay for the meal, and at a place like Jonah's it was bound to cost three or four times what it should. Then, again, Casta might really enjoy such an outing. But he wouldn't tell her about the tickets just yet. He wanted to make up his own mind about going first — without any outside pressure.

He found a note from her pinned to his favorite chair in the living room area.

"Be a little late, Tib. Stopping by the grocery." And, as always, she signed it simply: "C."

Smiling, he dropped the note on the floor and settled into the chair. "Tib." When had she started calling him that? She seldom did around others. It was her choice for a pet name.

"Hey-ey!"

He lifted heavy eyelids. He hadn't realized he'd been that drowsy.

"Hey-ey, Nate! Open this darn door."

He struggled over to the door and jerked it inward. There stood Casta, a bag of groceries in each arm.

"Well, darn you, ain't you gonna give me a hand with this stuff?"

Without comment, he reached out and took one of the bags from her and carried it to the kitchen, placing it on the sink cabinet beside the refrigerator.

"Boy, I'm wiped out. I hate shoppin' for groceries. Every time, it seems like I get in the aisles with the slowest checkers and the chattiest old bitches. If you want something to eat right away, you'll have to fix it yourself. I'm gonna lie down for a while."

"Yeah, that sounds good."

"Uh-uh. Don't start that, Nathan Tibbetts. I'm too tired for that stuff right now."

He ducked his head.

A few seconds later, she hugged him to her breast. "Oh, alright, you big baby. But can you let me rest for about ten minutes first?"

"Sure, Cass, whatever you say." Inside, he was grinning.

"Just wake me," she called as she struggled toward the bedroom.

Nate walked back into the living room area and seated himself again in his chair. He glanced down at his books on the floor beside him, and he thought about studying. However, he pulled the envelope out of the top book and examined the tickets again. Oh, what the hell, they'd go. Now, he could tell Casta.

It wasn't 10 minutes but closer to 30 minutes later when he woke her. He had never understood how anyone could get any rest in 10 minutes. It always took him a minimum of 15 to 20 to just get to sleep. But not so with Casta. If she were really tired, she could be asleep practically as soon as her head hit the pillow.

He lay down beside her and gently kissed her on the neck. He raised himself up slightly, but she didn't stir. Slipping his head down on his own pillow, he took in her classic beauty once again.

"Hey, ain't you gonna do that again?" she asked a few seconds later, opening her dark eyes and winking.

"Why you little... You were playing possum!"

She smiled. "I'm still waiting."

Nate bent over and kissed her on the neck once more, this time more aggressively.

"Hey, watch it, fellow. I said, 'Do it again,' but I'd like to have a neck when you get through."

"Oh, you would, would you?" He rolled her over onto her back and planted a gentle kiss on her lips. Her arms went around his neck, and she pulled him tightly against her, vigorously moving her hips in a rhythmic pattern. It was more than two minutes before she finally released him.

"Now, who's getting carried away?" he asked.

"Can I help it if you do these things to me?"

During the course of the next half hour, they went through a broad gamut of sensuous activity, each touching and being touched by more than the physical part of the other.

When it was over, Nate swung his legs off the bed and sat with his back to Casta. "I love you, you know," he said. "You mean more to me than anything I can imagine."

She rolled over next to him and began stroking a hand up and down the center of his back.

"I'm yours forever, Tib." She said, pausing briefly before continuing, "It's hard to believe we'll be gettin' married in just about a month, isn't it?"

He nodded.

Her hand halted its movement up and down his back, and she circled her arm around his body. He leaned back and embraced her once again. Seconds later, they were once more joined in the bond of love.

In the shower afterwards, he remembered the tickets, and he thought about calling out to her to tell her about them, but he decided against it. Maybe they really shouldn't go, anyway. How could he think about having fun at a time like this? Was he some heartless beast?

While he was drying off, Casta came into the bathroom with a mundane announcement, bringing him back to the reality of day-to-day existence.

"You're not going to believe this," she began, "but I've started making spaghetti sauce, and when I looked in the cabinet, I found we didn't have any spaghetti to go in it. I thought we had some or I woulda got some today when I'ze at the store. Would you be too mad if I asked you to run out and get some while I finish fixing everything else. Okay, Tib? I'd really appreciate it."

She stepped up to him and gave him a light peck on the lips. "I love you," she added.

"Bribery, huh?" He smiled. "Okay, it worked — *this* time. But just don't make a habit of it. Got that?"

Now, she grinned. "Just make sure it's vermicelli. I don't care what brand."

Nate dressed quickly. Spaghetti. Good, he loved

spaghetti. Mama used to make it all the time when Otis was alive. It was one of his favorites.

"If you don't quit eatin' so much a that, you gonna turn into a I-talyen," she told Otis.

"Oh, come on, Mama. I won't really, will I?" Otis asked. "Please can you fix it? Please."

Otis tugged at her skirt, and she looked down at him and smiled.

"Chile, what am I gonna do with you? Jus' call you my little I-talyen, I guess."

Nate stared silently. He'd wait and see how Brother made out. If Otis failed to persuade her, then he'd have to try.

"Mama, please. You make it so-o-o-o good," Otis continued.

"Okay, boy, I'll make your spaghetti, but we'll just haveta go out and git it, 'cause I ain't got none in th' house."

Otis began to jump up and down, still holding onto Mama's skirt tail. "Thank you, Mama! Thank you!"

She grabbed him up and planted a big kiss right on his lips, then she reached out and patted Nate on the top of his head. "Well, git your coats, boys, and let's go."

"Yippee!" Nate shouted.

He couldn't have been more than six or seven then, but it seemed like only yesterday.

"You got money, Tib?" Casta called from the kitchen.

"What?"

"I said, 'Do you need money?' If you do, just take some out of my purse. I think it's in the closet."

"No, I've got some. Shouldn't take much to buy a package of spaghetti, should it?" he asked, strolling into the kitchen, taking in the spicy aroma which pervaded the air. "Hm-m-m, smells good."

"Thanks, Hon. Just a coupla bucks ought to be

enough."

"Then, I'm fine."

He stepped up to where she stood at the stove, stirring the sauce, and gave her a light kiss on the cheek.

"See you in a few minutes."

It was already dark when he stepped outside, but the temperature must still be close to 80 and humid. Some long-range weather forecasts were already calling for this to be "a long, hot summer." He realized that that phrase had meant something different a generation before he was born. In the '60's and '70's, there had been several long, hot summers. By the '80's and the '90's, the 'hood was seeing many new African American-owned businesses, and the whites were moving their businesses out to the suburbs. Unfortunately, most of those black businesses, like Uncle Charlie's clothing store, weren't backed by much capital, and they couldn't withstand the lean years it took to get established. Uncle Charlie, like so many others, just never had a chance.

Nate pulled a handkerchief from his back pocket and wiped the sweat off his face. He wasn't going to hang around out here any longer than he had to, he decided, taking a short-cut to the nearest quick market. The alley he chose was almost pitch dark, but he'd been down it before in the daylight, and he knew his way well. Part of his mind was on the spaghetti Casta was going to fix for him, and part of it was drifting along in the past. So, when he heard the ruckus behind him, he figured it was just a cat digging through a garbage can, but it most definitely wasn't.

CHAPTER THREE

Still, something made him swing around — he didn't know what — and he could barely make out their hazy outlines. There were two of them, and one was big, almost a giant. In the darkness, Nate would swear the man was all of eight feet tall. They had been creeping toward him; however, when they realized he was now facing them, they picked up the pace.

"Now!" he heard the smaller one shout. Smaller one, that was a laugh. He must be several inches taller than Nate.

Nate jumped to the right just as he heard the "swoosh" of a knife cutting the air only inches from his face. Now, he ducked to the left, then shifted right again just as the giant came crashing past him. There was a good deal of clanging and clatter as the man smashed into a stack of garbage cans and litter.

Oh, God, these guys meant business, Nate realized. He squeezed his hands into fists and tried to relax his breathing to near normal, but he was unable to. Glancing down the alley, he realized that it was a long way to the next street, and even if he made it that far, there was no assurance these guys would leave him alone.

He tried to clear his throat, too, but with little success. "Wha-what do you want?"

No response.

"Money. You want my money, right? I don't have much, but you can have what I've got."

He started to reach for his back pocket, but he stopped short when he realized neither of the other men had yet spoken.

Slowly, Nate continued to inch backwards down the alley. Out of the corner of his left eye he could see the giant getting to his feet.

"Dammit! What is it you *want*?"

Still no response.

In desperation now, he turned and began to run as fast as his legs would carry him in the direction he had been traveling when the two had appeared behind him. But he didn't last long.

Suddenly he went tumbling forward on his face, and a split second later, he heard a loud "yelp." A dog had evidently been sleeping in the alley, probably trying to keep cool by lying on the concrete. Nate could hear his adversaries closing ground behind him, so he rolled quickly away from the center of the alley just as a huge body landed beside him.

He pulled himself up as fast as his aching muscles would allow, but something had snagged his right foot. It was the giant, he knew, lying prone at his feet. With all the effort he could muster, Nate swung and planted his shoe where the other man's face should be. There was an "oof," and he felt his leg released.

And not a second too soon, for the other man was closing on him with the knife. There was a glint of light off it as the blade swung past him several times, Nate barely avoiding contact each time through the random movement of his nimble feet. Finally, he ducked under one blow and began running back in the direction from which he had just come. But he could hear the other hard on his heels.

Abruptly, Nate leaped to one side and stuck out a foot. His timing was almost perfect. His pursurer went crashing against the hard pavement.

However, his luck didn't hold out for long. His eyes had adjusted to the dark and he could see the giant closing.

Glancing back at the fallen man with the knife, Nate saw he, too, had begun to rise and move toward him.

And Nate knew he was trapped between them!

The sweat was dripping off his face, and he tried hard to swallow whatever that was in his throat, but it refused to go down.

"For Christ's sake," he shouted, "why are you doing this?" But the other two were as silent as before.

The man with the knife made another lunge at Nate, who had

no choice but to fade back toward the big man. The blade man, this time, stayed close on his heels, and, before he realized it, Nate found himself driven almost into the bigger man's arms. Just as the giant reached out to grab him, Nate took a desperate gamble and threw himself flat at the other's feet.

"A-a-a-a-ay!"

The scream came from the giant. Nate watched as the knife plunged deep into his massive chest.

Nate had to move quickly to get out of the way of the falling body, then scramble to his feet again before the other man could reach him with the knife he had retrieved from his partner.

Now the odds were more even, and, though he had never been a fighter, Nate decided to stand his ground and watch for an opening. The other had been vulnerable to a trip, so he tried this first. However, his adversary easily outstepped him and took another swipe at him with the knife, this time coming very close to his chest.

Back upright, Nate joined the other in a circling motion as each looked for a way to bring down his opponent. They continued like this for more than a minute until the other man decided to make his move, and that was his undoing. Again, Nate sidestepped the blade, and, as the man passed him bent low in a crouch, Nate clenched his hands together in a double fist and brought them down hard against the back of the other's neck. The man went crashing to the pavement, striking his head, and the knife went skidding away down the alley.

Exhausted, Nate found that he could no longer stand either, and he crumbled down to a sitting position beside his fallen foe. His breath was coming in gasps, and drenched in sweat, he was shivering, despite the heat.

A sound — a low moan — caught his attention, and he glanced over at the man lying less than three feet away from him. Nate could see a slight movement of the chest. His mind told him to stand, that he must get up, but his body refused to budge. There simply was no energy left to permit movement. He needed rest. He needed to lie down here and rest, but his mind said, "No."

The war between body and mind raging within him never had a chance to resolve itself, for, without further warning, the man who had had the knife sprang from the pavement and launched himself toward Nate's listless form. He tried to avoid the on-coming projectile, but he had not the strength. The other man's shoulder caught him full in the chest and knocked him backwards. Now, his opponent was sitting astride him, pounding away at his face with lead fists. Nate tried to block the blows with his arms and elbows, but with little effect. And he found he couldn't reach the other's face to even attempt to return the blows. He felt himself becoming increasingly groggy with each delivery from the other's fists, but, somehow, the pain of the blows did not overwhelm him. His face had almost become numb to the hurt.

His only hope, he realized suddenly, was to somehow get this beast of a man off him and force his legs to work and try to outrun the other. Even standing toe-to-toe he had no chance in a slugfest. Grabbing his right fist in his left hand, he pulled it back as far as he could, then shoved the elbow hard into the other man's mid-section. He could feel the air go out of his adversary as he did. So he repeated the effort. And again and again. Suddenly, the pounding by the other's fists stopped, but Nate found the strength to shove his elbow into the man one more time — with even more effort than he had exerted before.

The other crumbled off him, and Nate forced his leg muscles to work. Seconds later, he found himself standing. He had no idea how he'd accomplished the feat, just that he had. And he found that he could still run, as he made his way back down the dark alley, then the street leading to his apartment.

Nate didn't know if he was being pursued, and he wasn't about to let himself break gait long enough to look behind him.

But one thing he did know: That *twice in the last three days* he had only narrowly escaped the clutches of death!

CHAPTER FOUR

Slam.

Click.

Listen.

But he heard nothing. Pressing his ear against the door, he attempted to pick up any sounds emanating from just outside his apartment.

Then there was something.

Tap.

Tap.

Tap.

Was it the sound of a man climbing the stairs? The sound of shoes with metal plates striking the hard wood of the stairs?

Tap.

Tap.

Then it stopped.

Was someone standing just outside his door? A man with a knife ready to pick his lock and strike him down?

Nate pressed his ear more firmly against the door. Why wasn't it equipped with a peephole? They didn't cost much. But his landlord was too damn cheap. There were no frills here.

He strained his ears, and he heard something else.

Bump.

Bump.

Bump.

What was that? What was going on out there?

Swish.

Swish.

And —

"Nate? Is that you? Can you bring the spaghetti in here?" What?

Oh, the spaghetti. Now he remembered.

Casta strolled into the darkened living room holding a wooden spoon full of sauce.

"Here, you want to taste — hey, what you doing?"

He threw a forefinger up to his lips. "Sh-h-h-h!"

"What?"

"Dammit, Cass just *be quiet*!"

She slumped down onto the sofa, still holding the spoon, a quizzical look on her face.

Nate pressed his ear even more tightly against the door. Nothing.

No more sounds.

A few seconds later, he moved away from the door and slumped into his chair.

"Whew!"

"Are you gonna tell me what this is all about? And where's the spaghetti?"

He held up his right hand, his fingers spread wide apart. "Just a minute, okay? Gimme a minute."

Casta sat still staring at him, but she offered no further comment.

Finally, Nate stood again and walked slowly back over to the apartment door. He bent and put his ear against it again. A few seconds later, he raised up, flipped the lock and threw the door open.

The hallway was empty.

He closed the door, securing the lock once again, then moved over to the couch and dropped down beside Casta.

"I'm sorry..."

"*Now*, will you tell me what's going on?"

Nate nodded. "I was almost killed — that's all!"

"What?"

"Two thugs waylaid me in the alley. I think one of them's dead."

"Dead?" She sounded like an echo.

"Yeah. One of 'em had a knife and tried to stab me with it. The other was a gorilla who tried to catch me so he could squeeze me to death. He almost did too, but I ducked just in time, and the other guy's knife got him in the heart."

"Oh, God!" She bent over, holding a hand over her mouth.

"But I got away. I don't think I was followed." Liar. Why was he lying to her?

"Then why all that listening at the door?"

Stupid. If he was going to lie, he should at least try to be more convincing. "Oh, that? Well, I, uh, I can't be sure." Good. Now, he felt much better.

She put the spoon down on the floor and reached out to hug him.

"Oh!"

"What it it?"

"Just sore, I guess."

Slowly, she slipped her hands away from his chest and face. "What did they do to you?"

Nate dropped his head backward onto the top of the couch. "One of 'em — the one with the knife — he pinned me down — "

"God, Nate, did he stab you? Are you — ?"

"No, not that. He never touched me with the blade. I'd already knocked it out of his hand. He just sat on top of me and gave me one hell of a beating, that's all."

"That's all?"

"Come on, Cass. You know what I mean: It's just that he

didn't cut me. I'm alright — except for a lot of bruises."

"My poor baby. Why don't you go in the bedroom and lie down?
I'll bring some ice."

He did as she had instructed, and within five minutes he was lying on the bed, holding one while she held two ice packs to his face, head, and body.

"Thank God that's all." She bent over and gently kissed him between the ice packs. "You're lucky you're even alive." He nodded assent, but said nothing.

"The cops. Maybe we better call the cops and tell them about it and about that dead man, don't you think?" she asked after several moments of silence.

She stood up, but Nate grabbed her arm and shook his head. "No, don't, Casta!"

"Why not?"

"Uh, it's just, uh, my word against his — the one with the knife."

"But they jumped you. Anybody can see — "

"No! I said, 'No!' and I mean it. I think they were white, and you know the cops ain't gonna believe two whites jumped a black kid in an alley and tried to kill him."

"But — "

"No, buts! No telling what might happen if you call in the cops. They might even charge me with murdering that bastard. Just let it lie, okay?"

She offered him a tentative smile. There was silence for several minutes more, then she tried a new approach.

"What if they find him in that alley and trace it to you? Won't you be worse off then?"

Nate thought for a moment. "Probably. But how they gonna do that? It was dark and — "

"What? After the way you came running in here! Don't you think maybe somebody saw you?"

He shook his head. "Don't know. Could be. But I'm not gonna be the one to call the cops in. Please, Casta, drop it. Please?"

"Okay, Tib. Anything you say... Oh, I just thought of something: I could say you was with me all the time, that you never left the apartment, that — "

"No, like you said: Somebody mighta seen me runnin'?"

"How about that I was with you then and that they jumped me and you fought them off?"

"Casta, no! Don't worry about it. Thee cops'll probably never trace it to me anyway. And if they do..."

"If they do, what?"

He shrugged, and at last she fell silent.

For more than an hour, he lay there with the ice packs pressed against his skin. Finally, he decided he wanted to sleep more than anything else. Casta took away the ice, and, despite the aching and the throbbing, he soon found himself dozing off.

He could see Mama standing in the doorway, and he was running toward her. Just before he reached her, he had second thoughts and pulled himself to a halt.

"Sonny, what's that all over you? Come here!"

Nate moved toward her in slow, measured steps.

"Now!" she bellowed, and he thought his eardrums would surely burst.

He closed the gap between them in a few seconds. She bent down — and screamed.

"Blood!"

She seemed to be panting for breath.

She repeated the word as she examined his face, then her breathing became more regular.

"Nathan Michael Tibbetts" — he hated it when she called him by his full name; it was a sure sign he was in trouble — "you want to tell me what happened?"

"Uh, Mama, it was Otis' fault. He pushed me — "

"Brother? Where is he?"

"He's, uh, back there, Mama." He swung and pointed in the direction from which he had just come. Just barely, he could make out his brother's hazy image.

Mama stood upright and looked in Otis' direction. She cupped her hands around her lips and began to yell.

"Otis. O-o-o-tis. Richard Otis Tibbetts, you come here, right this minute!"

Nate could see his brother begin to run toward them.

"Mama," he pleaded, "it wudn't my fault. It was — "

She took one of her hands and cupped it over his mouth. "Hush, chile. I don't want to hear it."

He could already hear Otis bellowing. "Mama, Nate hit me. He hit me in th' face. I wudn't doin' nuthin' and he hit me. Honest, Mama."

When his brother was standing beside him, she silenced Otis, too.

"I ain't gonna hear no more 'bout this, you hear me?"

They both nodded. Was she going to let them get by with it?

No! She took them both by the arms and led them inside. From the top of the refrigerator she removed that old Bolo paddle without the ball and rubber band and gave each more licks than Nate cared to count.

After that, when he and Otis fought, they kept it to themselves, never again reporting it to Mama, no matter how badly one of them was hurt. If blood was spilled, they cleaned themselves up. If they had brusies to show for their battles, they always blamed them on a fall or a bump or something like that.

"Tib? Tib?"

He felt soft fingers on his arms and he opened his eyes. "Yeah? Wha — ?" He sat up, shaking his head.

On the bed, sitting beside him, was Casta, still fully clothed.

"Cass, I had this terrible dream that two men — " but he halted his words as he ran his fingers across the bruises on his face.

She smiled gently and stroked his arm.

"Oh," he added finally, "I guess it wasn't a dream, after all."

Casta shook her head. "I made you some soup. You never did get anything to eat tonight."

Now, he realized that she had been holding a bowl in her other hand, all along.

"Oh, yeah, I guess I am a little hungry. What time is it, anyway?"

"A little past two. I've been studying for a history exam. I was about to turn in when I decided you might like to have something."

She raised the spoon to his lips.

The warm soup went down soothingly.

"M-m-m-m," he said, nodding. "Cheese!"

"Yep. I made it myself from scratch. Nothing's too good for my man."

Nate smiled. "Thanks, Cass. I love you, you know."

"Well, you better. I don't want to waste my time making cheese soup for somebody who doesn't."

"You're too good for me."

Smiling, she nodded. "Maybe. But you'll get your chance to be good to me pretty soon."

"How long is it?" She would know what he meant.

She looked up for a moment, as if she were thinking. "It's five weeks, three days, sixteen hours, and, uh, forty-three minutes, and some odd seconds. Is that close enough?"

He smiled. "And then you'll be Mrs. Tibbetts."

Casta glanced away for a second, then when she looked back, he could see a touch of moisture in her eyes.

"I've been meaning to talk to you about that, Nate."

She paused and looked away again.

"Well...?" he prompted, finally.

She turned and looked into his eyes once more. "Well, I've been thinking. Would you mind terribly if I didn't change my last name? I'll still be your wife and all. Nothing else would be different."

His smile disappeared briefly, but he managed to prop it back up. "So what's the big deal?" he asked.

"Good. I knew you'd understand, Tib. It's just that I've been Casta Jordan all my life. I don't see why I should change that. Why should the wife take the man's name any more than the man take the wife's? It really doesn't make any sense when you think about it. If there's got to be a name change, why can't both spouses just agree on a third — kind of neutral — name? Oh, I know, I know, there would be problems in tracing genealogy, maybe, and stuff like that? But the old way's just a sexist extension that society continues to permit, don't you think?"

"Yeah, maybe. I've never really thought about it," Nate responded. "But if you don't want to change your last name, I don't know any reason you should. I'll still love you the same whether you're Casta Jordan or Casta Tibbetts. You'll always be my Casta."

She put the almost-empty bowl of soup on the night stand and bent down and kissed him. "I love you, too. And thanks, Tib, for seeing my side." She paused again briefly, then resumed. "But if you want me to become Mrs. Tibbetts, just tell me. I'll — "

"Look, Cass, it ain't no biggie. Okay."

She smiled again, snuggling dawn beside him. He could feel her warm breath on his shoulder, and there was a stirring inside him. He pulled her to him and kissed her passionately. Gently, he began to stroke her soft, C-cup breast through the fabric of her blouse.

"Again?" she whispered in his right ear.

"Oh, Casta, I love you so much."

He shifted his hand lower on her body.

Suddenly, she sat up and pulled away from him.

"No, better not!"

"What? What's the matter, baby? Not afraid of wearing it out, are you? Won't happen. It comes with a lifetime guarantee, and no matter how hard you try, it just bounces right back."

"Stop it, Nate. Quit kiddin' around." She took his hand and removed it from her breast.

"Okay, if that's the way you want it." He slumped back down on his pillow.

"Come on, Nate, can't you see what I'm saying. You just nearly got beat to death out there tonight. You've got bruises all over your body. Why can't you just rest?"

"I'm alright, Casta. Do I look dead to you?"

"Cut it out." She jumped up and grabbed the bowl off the nightstand, stomping out of the room.

Christ, woman! What was the matter with her? Couldn't she see he needed her now? Sometimes he had a feeling that she had no real appreciation of his needs. It just went to show that men and women were still different, no matter what the experts said. Men still craved sex; they had to have it to satisfy their animal urges. But women were different. Sometimes he had the feeling they could just take it or leave it. Other drives still seemed to override the need to copulate. And one of these was the maternal instinct. He knew he'd just seen a prime example of this.

"Okay, you sex fiend. Here I come, ready or not!" he heard Casta shout from the living room, just before she burst into the bedroom completely nude, smiling broadly. She threw herself down beside him. "Well, what's the holdup? Aren't you a little overdressed for the occasion?" she asked as she began to unbutton his shirt.

Damn! And just when he had women all figured out!

INTERLUDE B

"How did it happen this time?"

"I went with the simple and direct, and it failed. I lost a man in the operation."

"An expendable?"

"Yes, I'm using only expendables. I feel it's too risky to further involve myself at this point. He might get suspicious."

"I concur with your judgment, Panther."

"Thank you, sir."

"How is this affecting his emotional stability?"

"I'm unable to make an adequate analysis at this point.
I've had no direct contact with him since the incident."

"But you are keeping in close touch?"

"Yes, sir, I am."

"What about your next operation? Do you have it in mock up yet?"

"To tell the truth, sir, I'm having some reservations about the whole procedure."

"You are?"

"Yes. I'm not certain we're employing the most effective approach with him."

"I see."

"But I don't believe my feelings will affect my ability to carry out the operation. I simply felt I should inform you, Cougar."

"I appreciate that. I'm going to have to clear this line, now. I have another important call coming in. Perhaps we should discuss this in more detail later. I don't think I have to tell you how valuable you are to this endeavor, do I, Panther? It's much too late to replace you. You understand that, don't you?"

"Perfectly, sir."

CHAPTER FIVE

The aroma of bacon cooking was the first thing he noticed when he opened his eyes.

Slowly, he sat up, and, as he did so, the stiffness in and around his muscles made itself known. A hand shot up to check his face, and he found that most of the puffiness was gone. He struggled into the bathroom to relieve himself, and he could see that there was still some swelling around his eyes and nose but hardly enough to distort his features.

She was already making omelets by the time he got to the kitchen.

"Mornin'," he said, and she whirled around.

"What are you doing outa bed, Mr. Tibbetts?"

"Ah, gimme a break, Casta, Don't start that stuff again."

"If *that stuff* means I'm concerned about you, then I'm gonna start." She stuck out her lower lip, then turned back to her cooking. "How do you feel?" she added, finally.

"Stiff and sore, but I'll live."

"Sounds to me like you're *damn* lucky to be alive."

"Yeah, that's true."

"So why don't you just scramble right on back into that bed. I'll bring your breakfast in to you when it's ready."

"Now, Cass, it's not that serious."

"Not that serious? You were nearly beat to death, and you don't call that serious? I'd like to know what you do call serious."

"Sure, it was serious, but I can't stop my whole life just because a coupla thugs try to do me in. Can I?"

"Well, no, not exactly."

She took the omelets out of the skillet and took the skillet off the ancient stove, then she walked over to its refrigerator counterpart and removed a carton of milk. She poured two glasses full and served up two plates of bacon and omelets, placing Nate's portion in front of him.

"Besides, I've got to get some reading done this morning before I go to Simmons' class," Nate added, after several moments of silence.

"You're gonna do what?"

"Study! Ever hear of it?"

She drew her face up in a disgusted pout. "No, the other part: Did I hear you say that you're going to classes today."

"Sure, why not?"

She stood and left the room, without offering further comment. Nate sat silently, finishing his breakfast. Casta was an excellent cook and great company most of the time — except when she got on her "high horse." Then there was just no living with her. Things had to be her way, or no way at all.

While he was standing at the leaky, dingy sink rinsing out his plate and glass, he heard the toilet flush, and shortly Casta came back into the room.

"Listen, Cass," he began, "sure, I'm a little banged up, but I do have other things to think about — like finishing my education."

She said nothing, but just began to scrape her practically untouched food into the garbage. The glass of milk went down the sink.

Okay, if that was the way she wanted it, he could play the same way. He shaved and showered quickly and got dressed. There was no possibility of concentrating here, so he gathered up his books and papers and made his way to the front door. When he reached it, he paused and called out to her.

"I'm going now, Casta. I'll see you tonight." And he jerked the door open and stormed out, slamming it behind him.

At a study table in the library, he spread his things around and opened up his biology text. For more than ten minutes he stared at one page before he realized his eyes were not transmitting the message to the brain, or rather that the brain was not bothering to decipher it. He knew that there was more on his mind than his quarrel with Casta and his run-in with the thugs, but he didn't want to focus on it. He had to study, he told himself.

After a few minutes, he closed the biology book and got out French literature, one of his favorites. This should get him started off if anything would.

Nothing.

Another fifteen minutes wasted. Christ! Come on mind, get to work. He knew there was something up there. His intelligence had displayed itself a few times in the past. No use playing cat and mouse now. Come on out and get busy.

Still nothing.

A noise nearby attracted his attention, and he glanced up to observe a curvaceous young woman with brown hair and blue eyes picking up a pencil off the library floor. Nate realized almost immediately that her eyes were riveted on him. He tried to look away when their eyes met, but he couldn't. She smiled broadly and slowly retrieved the pencil. Finally, she broke her stare as she stood. Nate watched almost hypnotized as she moved away from him, swaying hips in her satiny-finish, tight-fitting dress.

He smiled slightly and shook his head. Women! They didn't make it easy for a college guy. Either they were driving you to distraction or telling you off.

Out of the corners of his eyes he saw that it was almost ten, so he stacked his books, grabbed them up, and left the library.

Although he was on time for Simmons' French lit class and answered roll when it was called, his mind never was present. Biology was equally a wipeout. In a daze, he arrived for Alland's class, and, of course, Alland didn't bother with attendance. He never did. Instead, he dived immediately into one of his tirades. This one was on the inadequacy of Virgil when compared to Homer.

At least it got Nate's attention. But not for long.

"Really like to read, don't ya, Sonny?"

He looked up and smiled at Mama.

"Yeah," he said, glancing back down at Velikovsky's *Worlds in Collision.*

"That 'nuther one of them science fiction books?"

"No, Mama. It's just science."

In bed, he was lying on his stomach, raised up on his elbows, and Mama stepped over next to him and ran her fingers through his hair.

"Betcha Brother woulda been like you, too. I 'member he couldn't get 'nough of them comic books."

"Yeah, we useta swap for all kinds of 'em, Mama. But Otis always got the best ones. Guess he was just good at swappin'."

"You still miss your brother a lot, don't ya?"

"Yeah, Mama, I do. Even though it's been four years. I guess ..."

"Uh-huh. It's been nearly thirteen years since your daddy died, and I still wake up at night thankin' he's layin' there beside me. Don't guess I'll ever get over that.

"Mama, did you ever think about gettin' married again?"

She shifted her gaze away from him. "Guess I wouldn't be tellin' you th' truth if I said I didn't. Uh-huh, I thought 'bout it a lot. Sometimes I get really lonely raisin' you by myself, 'specially since Brother died. I guess I never felt like any other man could ever take your daddy's place, that's all."

"I see, Mama." He cleared his throat. "Course nobody could take Daddy's place, like nobody could ever take Otis' place, but still you might want to think about it someday. After all — well, I, uh, been thinkin' about going to college when I graduate from high school. What do you think?

"I think you don't want me livin' here all by myself."

"That's true, Mama. I would feel a lot better if...if — "

"Jus' don't worry 'bout me, Sonny. I can take care of myself.

I have for more'n ten years now, and I've practically raised you."

"Okay. You win, Mama. But I just wanted you to know that it's alright with me if you, if — well, if you want to get married again."

"You mean I got your permission?"

"Yeah, Mama, you sure have," he said, smiling broadly.

She stopped stroking his hair and turned and strolled out of his room. He watched until she was out of sight, then he went back to *Worlds in Collision*.

But she never remarried.

He could see that Alland was still ranting in front of the class, but he had long since tuned out the words. A trail of tears had migrated out of the corners of his eyes and was making its way down his cheeks. *He had to stop blaming her*. She wasn't leaving him because she wanted to any more than Daddy or Otis had left because they wanted to. But somewhere in the back of his mind, he knew he'd been thinking that.

Oh, Mama, can you forgive me?

It had been six days now since he'd learned about her cancer, and not once since then had he allowed himself to set foot in that hospital again. Mama was lying there dying — she might die almost any day — and he hadn't even been by to see her. Why? How could he have abandoned her when she needed him so much? What kind of beast had he become?

College! Education! Crap — all crap. His Mama was lying in a hospital bed across town dying of cancer and he was sitting here listening to a madman spout gibberish.

Grabbing his books up in a massive disarray, he was just climbing to his feet when the first twinges of the headache struck.

"Mr. Tibbetts!" he heard someone shout, and he turned to stare at Alland. "You have an important engagement elsewhere, do you? You can't stay for the remainder of today's discussion of Virgil, you say?"

The hammers were beginning to rip into his skull, but he knew he had to say something.

"Oh, I, uh — "

"Sit down, Mr. Tibbetts, you can wait to make your departure along with everyone else, I'm sure."

Crashing. Clanging. Tearing into his brain. He raised his left hand and applied pressure to his temple, but it had little effect.

"Dr. Alland, you see — "

"Mr. Tibbetts, I said, 'Sit down!' You're disrupting the entire class."

He knew the hammers had to be tearing into gray matter inside his head, ripping it apart. He felt like screaming, but he stood here listening to a pinheaded jerk make fun of him.

"Dr. Alland, I have to — "

"Tibbetts — !"

Nate raised his voice. "I said that I *have* to go!"

"You mean you can't hold it until the end of this period? It's only...let me see...another 12 minutes. Surely you can hold on another 12 minutes. Or, are you leaving for another reason? Please tell us, Mr. Tibbetts, why you think it's so important that you depart at this very moment."

A saw! A saw had joined the hammers, and it was slicing off the top of his head.

"Dammit, man," he shouted, "I've got to go *because* my mother is dying!" With that, he swung around, not waiting to see if Alland could come up with another witty remark. He charged out of the classroom door at a near run, but that was as far as he got.

Now, there was a whole workshop inside his head: hammers, saws, drills, sanders, and everything else. And all were racing at full speed. He could feel the hallway rocking from side-to-side, and the people walking toward him looked twisted and misshapened.

Christ! His head felt as though it were about to explode as his books went flying and he slid down to the hallway floor and leaned back against the wall.

Then, abruptly, he was plunged into total darkness.

CHAPTER SIX

A train went rumbling by. Nate could make out the bump-bump, clackety-clack. He'd always had a fascination for trains — so big, so powerful. Otis and he used to stand and watch the trains go by, making noises and calling out to workmen aboard the mighty locomotives.

But there was no whistle. He heard no whistle. Why didn't this train have a whistle?

In fact, the clacking didn't sound exactly right either. It sounded more like a shuffle — not a train sound, at all. The sound was more like —

Dozens of feet!

Nate pried his eyelids open and stared around him, trying to get his bearings. He saw a mass of legs passing by him. He was just at knee level. His back was against the wall.

Now, it began to return to him. He knew where he was.

Mama!

He'd been thinking about Mama — about going to her — when the headache it.

Slowly, using the wall for support, he began to rise. When he was fully erect, he put a hand to his forehead to massage it, to feel the place where the headache had been. That headache — the worse headache he'd ever had in his life — was now gone completely! Not a twinge of pain remained.

The crowd of students hurrying from one classroom to the next had all but dissipated, so he began to look around the floor for his books and belongings. He found everything scattered about within a half-dozen feet of where he had been sitting – everything but his text for Alland's class. Even after the hall had completely cleared, he saw no sign of it. Oh, well, maybe it would show up later. Maybe one of the other students had picked it up and would return it to him tomorrow. Perhaps, in his haste, he'd left it inside the classroom. He thought about going back inside to check, but he didn't really want to chance seeing Alland again right now — not after the exchange of a few moments ago — and the man might still be inside.

Anyway, he had something important to do. He couldn't postpone it any longer.

Waiting at the bus stop ten minutes later, he thought about his old '92 Olds, wishing again he had the money to get it repaired. But it needed too much work, and, besides, he couldn't really afford to gas it up. Maybe after graduation he should just take a job — a *good* job — and forget about continuing his education. Maybe then his new bride and he could afford a good car, one that didn't drink money.

The bus was late, and he had to transfer once, but less than an hour later, he was walking into St. Thaddeus Memorial Hospital. His mother's room was on the sixth floor, and, when he entered, he found her asleep. One of the nurses had seen him about to go in and had cautioned him to "Keep your visit brief. She needs her rest." Rest, hell! What for? Did she need to rest up to die?

"Hi, Mama," he said quietly, grasping her limp hand.

She opened her eyes. "Sonny! I been worried 'bout you. Where you been?"

Worried about him — just like Mama. "I, uh, I been studying up for a big test, Mama. I got some big tests comin' up, soon. So I can graduate on time."

She smiled at him and stared deeply into his eyes. "That's fine, Sonny. Good. I mighta knowed it. You was always such a good studier." She squeezed his hand.

"Yeah, Mama, I been working hard..." Liar! How could he stand here lying to her like this? She knew. She must know. Mama could always tell when he was lying.

"Sonny, I want you to promise me something." He could feel the strength draining out of her grip.

"Sure, Mama. What is it?"

"Promise me you'll always keep your studies up. No matter what happens, don't give up your learnin'."

No matter what happens! She knew! Didn't she? But he hadn't told her. Had that son-of-bitching doctor told? Nate had made him promise not to, but had he done it anyway?

"I been layin' here thankin' 'bout how good you always been in school, and it serves me proud. You a good boy, Sonny. Sometimes, I don't tell you that, but I jus' want you to know."

She knew! She really knew. Dammit, why hadn't that damn doctor spared her this anguish? Why burden her with worry when she had such a short time left?

He cupped her hand in both of his and stroked it softly. "Thanks, Mama."

"Well, you know, I jus' had a lotta time to thank 'bout this while I been a-layin' here in this hospital bed. Couldn't go no place. Nothin' to do, 'cept watch TV, and you get tired a that, 'specially with this reality TV junk they have on now. No, I jus' wanted to tell you that before I get outa here, that's all."

Before she got out! Maybe she didn't know, after all.

"Mama, you didn't really have to tell me that. I knew how you felt."

"Maybe so, but sometimes I don't always let you know 'bout how I feel — 'specially after Brother died."

He glanced away. Maybe she knew, and maybe she didn't; he wasn't certain.

"Well, now, Sonny. How 'bout Casta? How she doin'?"

"Good, Mama. She's fine." He looked back toward her, trying to hold back his tears. "She, uh, sends her love. Said she'd be by to see you later."

Mama attempted another weak smile. "That would be nice. You bring her next time you come. You know she's a good girl, Sonny. You keep her. Don't let nothin' come 'tween you two, okay?"

"No, Mama, I won't."

"I mean it — not ever."

"I won't Mama. That's a promise, too." What about that fight they'd had just this morning? How many wedges like that did it take to split a relationship in two?

Mama answered his unspoken question. "Oh, boy, don't you thank there won't be arguments sometimes. There always is. You jus' has to learn *how* to argue, like me and your daddy done before we got married. You haveta be able to say what's on your mind without hurtin' the other person. That's the secret to a good marriage. I know me and your daddy woulda had a good, long one if it hadn't been for..."

Her voice trailed off, and she looked away from him. "Thanks, Mama. I think I see what you mean. You have to give the other party a chance to save face."

She turned her head and looked into his eyes again. "Face? Oh, yeah, that's right. They has to be able to come out okay, too, if that's what you mean."

"Right," he said, patting her hand once more.

"You gonna be a good husband, Sonny. I jus' know it. A good husband and a good daddy to your young-uns. I jus' wish I was gonna be..." Her voice trailed off again.

There was no use fooling himself anymore, Nate decided. She must have figured it out herself. She knew, and he knew she knew.

But he didn't have to acknowledge it, did he?

"Mama, we gonna have a whole house full of grandkids for you. They gonna keep you so-o-o busy you won't have time to sit down."

"I'd like that, boy. I jus' wish I could believe it."

"Would you cut it out, Mama?"

She took her free hand and pointed toward the small, metal cabinet beside the head of her bed. "I'm kinda thirsty, Sonny. Would you pour me a glass a water?"

He slipped his hands free of hers and stepped over to the cabinet and poured the water without further comment. Glancing around the room, his eyes paused when they came to the room's one other bed, which sat empty.

"What happened to your roommate?" he asked, handing her the glass of water.

"Gone. Th' first one's gone home. Th' second one's jus' gone. Took her away this mo'nin'. I tried to find out 'bout her. I asked the nurses, but they wouldn't say nothin'. But I know; I know. She died in her sleep last night, that's what."

"Oh."

"Don't be sad 'bout it, Sonny. She was a old lady, nearly 'bout seventy-five or eighty. And she was ready to meet her Lord. She was ready...like I am."

"Mama! I wish you'd quit telling yourself stuff like that. You're gonna be fine."

"Is that so? Then tell me what's wrong with me. What is it?"

"Uh, it's..."

"Cancer! I know."

"Why, that damn doc..." He bit his upper lip, trying to suppress the words.

"It's okay, Sonny. It wudn't Dr. Dryden that tole me. I just figured it out."

He tried to relax his facial muscles, but with little success. "Okay, Mama, so it's cancer. So what? Did you know that more than half of all cancer victims are cured?" Actually, the figure was closer to a third, but he felt like stretching it just a little.

"'Zat right?"

"Yeah, Mama. It is. With today's modern medicine, just because they say you have cancer doesn't mean you have to look forward to a lifetime of suffering or...or..."

"Or dyin' from it?"

He nodded.

"I know 'bout that stuff, Sonny. But this ol' *dinosaur* is ready to meet her Maker, if that's what he wants."

Christ! He just wished he could accept her passing so readily. Or did he? No, he didn't want to accept it. For, he knew, if he accepted it, he would be giving in. He would be handing her over. He would be saying, "Here she is: Come and get her." And he would never do that. There must be some way. There must be some cure, some miracle drug they simply hadn't tried yet. He just couldn't stand back and let death come and take Mama away without a fight.

Tears were forming in his eyes and trickling down his dark-brown cheeks.

She took his hand again and pulled it to her own cheek. "It's alright, Sonny. Don't cry for me."

Oh. Mama. You can't leave me. Please don't leave me. I'll find a way. Honest, I will.

"Mrs. Tibbetts?" he heard someone say, and he whirled to
see a frail, blonde nurse standing in the doorway to his mother's room. The nurse walked over and stood beside Mama, on the opposite side of the bed from him. "Mrs.

Tibbetts, it's time to check your signs again."

She looked up at Nate. "Would you mind waiting out in the hallway for a few minutes?"

At first, he just stood outside the room waiting for the nurse to complete whatever it was she was doing with Mama, but the moments ticked by, and still the young woman had not emerged. Finally, he strolled down to the sixth floor visitor's room where he found several vending machines. He deposited the coins, punched up a Pepsi, then downed it quickly.

Glancing at his watch, he noticed that it was almost 4:30. Even if he left right now, Nate knew it would be well after 5 before he could reach his apartment.

When he returned to his mother's room, the nurse was just completing her work. On the way out, she paused and whispered to Nate: "Please don't stay too much longer. She really needs to rest, now."

He nodded slightly and stepped back over to his mother's bedside.

She reached out to him and offered a brave smile, a smile that bridged a decade in his mind. Only back then he'd been the one lying in bed, tears soaking his young face. She stood beside him, offering that smile. But he didn't want her to smile. He didn't want anyone to ever smile again.

"Chile, I won't say it'll be alright, 'cause it won't. But we jus' has to go on."

"Mama, why?"

"Lord only knows, chile, why He took Brother 'way. It was jus' his time, that's all."

"No, Mama!" Nate shouted, sitting up, an angry look embedded in his facial muscles. "It wudn't his time! Otis was just ten. How could it be *his* time?"

"Sonny," she said, trying to hug him, while Nate rolled
away to avoid her arms, "we jus' never know when the

Lord's gonna call for us. We jus' has to be ready whenever he calls. Th' Good Book says we know neither the hour nor th' day. That's why we has to be ready all th' time. You understand?"

"No, Mama! It ain't fair! Why did he take Otis, *now*?"

"I don't know, chile."

"Well, I ain't gonna be ready — ever! When he comes for me, I'm gonna fight him. He ain't gonna take me easy."

"Oh, chile, chile. What am I gonna do with you?"

He broke into violent sobbing and fell into her arms at last. She sat on the edge of his bed holding him for more than a half hour, while he alternately cried and murmured, "It ain't fair."

Finally, she released him and looked him full in the face.

"Listen, Sonny. It jus' you and me, now. We ain't got nobody else. You won't get over Brother dying no more'n I got over your daddy. We jus' has to go on living ourselves. We can mourn 'em, but we can't ever bring 'em back. They're gone — both of 'em. Gone for good. Now, there's just you and me, Sonny. From here on out, we only got each other. And I know you don't want to hear this, and maybe it ain't th' best time to say it, but someday, there'll just be you. I'll be gone, too. And when that time comes, you'll just have to go on livin' like we're doing now. Understand?"

He looked up into her big, dark eyes. "Oh, Mama, I couldn't never go on livin' if you died, too."

She squeezed him tightly again. "Chile, I ain't plannin' to leave you for a good, long time, yet. I plan to be around to help raise my grandkids, and then your grandkids."

There was another flood of tears, but, somehow, Mama had helped him see beyond the hurt.

But she wasn't going to live to see his grandchildren,

or even his children. Nevertheless, she still beamed that brave smile at him.

"Feeling any better, Mama?"

"What makes you think I'm feelin' bad, Sonny?"

"Uh, well, I, uh, guess I just thought..." Oh, Lord, how was he ever going to get out of this one? She came to his rescue. "They got me so doped up I don't feel no pain most of th' time."

He nodded, trying to think of something to say.

"And they come in here ever hour or two and check my temperture and ever'thang else, seems like," she added.

"They're just trying to help you get well, that's all."

She glanced away momentarily, looking out the window. Finally, she spoke again. "Looks like rain out there. Been rainin' today?"

"No, not yet, Mama. But I think it may be in the forecast. I haven't been keeping up with the news much lately."

"Could use some rain, you know. We — "

"Oh, Mama, I'm gonna have to run. The nurse wants you to rest, now. Why don't you just close your eyes and get some sleep before they bring your supper in?"

She rolled her head, facing toward him once more. Her smile had disappeared. "You won't wait 'nuther six days to come back and see me, will you?"

"No, Mama. No matter how much studyin' I have to do, I'll still make time to come by and see you every day. Okay?"

"That's fine." She reached out for his hand, took it, and pulled it to her lips. "But I don't want you to get yourself behind in your school work on account of me. You understand?"

He nodded slightly, trying to offer her the same brave smile she had given him only a few moments before.

Slipping his hand out of hers, he bent over and

planted a light kiss on her forehead. "Now, you rest, like the nurse said."

At the doorway, he paused and turned, still trying to look cheerful. He opened his mouth, but it was Mama who offered the final comment.

"Now, 'member what I tole you 'bout Casta. You take care a her, and she'll las' you a lifetime."

As he left her room, Nate understood what she meant. His mother was passing him, like the proverbial torch, to another.

INTERLUDE C

"So, Panther, your psychograph is confirmed?"

"Yes, sir. Physical manifestations of the genetic changes have become apparent in him, also."

"Then you must speed up your efforts."

"Right."

CHAPTER SEVEN

Two blocks from his apartment, he slowed and glanced down the alley where the previous evening the muggers had waylaid him. There was no sign of the body of the larger of the two; he knew intellectually that there wouldn't be, but he could not prevent himself from looking, anyway. Strolling up the alley and looking for bloodstains on the pavement also occurred to Nate. His watch said it was only 5:40; sunset and darkness were a long way off. The survivor of that encounter wasn't likely to jump him in broad daylight, even if he were hanging around now, watching the alley, Nate told himself. Still, he couldn't convince his feet to move in that direction.

As he stood and stared down the now-quiet alley, Nate slowly raised his right hand to his face and moved the fingertips about his dark skin. All the puffiness was now gone, but the soreness certainly wasn't. And for the first time, he realized Mama hadn't noticed his bruises — or, if she had, at least she'd kept quiet about them.

Finally, he pried his gaze away from the alley and continued in the direction of his apartment. That was the moment two of his books chose to slide from underneath his left arm and crash to the sidewalk. As Nate bent to retrieve them, he noticed the envelope sticking out from one of them.

The tickets! Of course, he'd forgotten all about the

tickets to Jonah's which Alland had given him yesterday. Hurriedly, he jerked the envelope open and examined the contents. The performance of *Our American Cousin* was tonight at eight. In just over two hours.

He drew the tickets up to his lips and kissed them eagerly, smiling broadly. Thank goodness. This could be a Godsend.

Suddenly he found himself running down the street, laughing out loud. Surely Casta couldn't still be mad at him when he told her that they were headed out for an evening at the theater. He'd just omit the part about Alland giving them to him, for the time being. No need to take chances on spoiling tonight's fun. Then he remembered the last thing that had occurred in Alland's class this afternoon, and it made him shudder slightly — but it wasn't enough to destroy his overall mood of gaity. He'd just go to Dr. Alland tomorrow and explain to him about his mother and about his headache. The old bastard would understand. He had to.

By the time he reached his apartment on the second floor of the building, the perspiration was dripping off him, and he could taste the saltiness on his lips as he stood fumbling with the key. Just as he was about to insert it, the door flew open, and Casta threw herself at him. They stood there in the hallway wrapped in a moist embrace for several minutes before Nate broke free and pulled her inside.

"I'm sorry, honey," she was saying even before he got the door closed. Nate was dying to make his announcement about the theater tickets, but he knew better than to interrupt her. "I really didn't mean to sound so ugly to you this morning."

Just as the door clicked shut, she grabbed him again, pressing her lips firmly against his and forcing him back up against the wall. One of her hands went down past his waist and began to massage him through his pants. Oh, God, it felt great. But, he realized, Caste was making it very difficult for him to make his announcement.

Finally, after almost five minutes, she released him and just in time to prevent him from him from exploding inside his clothes.

"Oh, Nate, I love you so much," she began, almost immediately. "I only did that because I was concerned about your health. You know that, don't you?"

He nodded. "Casta — "

"Nate, baby, I was so worried about you. You're so late. I was afraid that maybe that other guy got ahold of you and did you in." She burst suddenly into uncontrollable sobbing, sinking down onto the couch.

Nate slipped down beside her and held her tightly in his arms. Immediately, the sobbing ceased and Casta's facial features changed. Gone was the joyous beauty who had welcomed him home. Gone was the weeping lover who had feared for his safety. Replacing them was a demoness whose eyes burned with anger. "Then, where the *hell* were you — you *inconsiderate bastard?*" she screamed, leaping to her feet.

"Cass, baby, I — "

"Out with some wench, telling her what a bitch you're living with?"

God, how could she change so quickly?

"No, dammit!" he shouted back. "No! Now would you sit down and listen?"

"I might listen, but I don't care to sit down any more," she retorted.

Nate thrust both his hands out and, grabbing her upper arms, forced her back down on the couch. "Now, shut up!" he bellowed.

Casta did not offer to speak — or move.

"I was over at the hospital, visiting Mama; that's

where I was!"

Her eyes shifted away from his, but not before he caught a glimmer of the tears returning.

"Oh," she said softly.

"And she asked about you. She even told me how lucky I am to have a woman like you, Casta Jordan. And you want to know something?"

She looked up, inquisitiveness in her eyes, but she said nothing.

"I agreed with her," he continued, after a brief pause.

"Oh, Nate," and the flood of tears resumed. But this time he didn't hold her. After a few seconds, she got herself under control enough to continue. "I did it again. What can I say? I'm sorry, that's all. But why didn't you call me? Why didn't you let me know what you were doing — so I wouldn't worry my head off? You know how I worry."

Nate remembered the tickets, and he stepped over to the beat up walnut coffee table where he'd dropped his books. He pulled out the envelope and returned to her.

"Here," he said, handing it over without further comment.

She opened it quickly, then glanced up at him, smiling through the tears. Slowly, she stood and gave him another solid kiss.

When she broke, he caught his breath, then spoke again. "I didn't want to call you because I was afraid I would blurt it out," he lied. "I wanted to surprise you, sweetheart."

"Well, you sure have."

He grinned, still holding her around her tiny waist.

"But, Jonah's? Why Jonah? We've never been there. Isn't that a dinner theater? Why...?"

He pointed with the index finger of his right hand toward the tickets which she still held. "Notice the show's title."

"*Our American Cousin?*" She looked up into his face, staring blankly.

"It was the play that Lincoln was watching when Booth gunned him down. I thought you might appreciate its historical significance."

Now, recognition was dawning and showed in her eyes. "Oh, yeah. I think I remember."

"Well, whether you do or not, you'd better start gettin' ready. It starts in about two hours."

"*Okay*, Tib." She whirled around, but before she stepped away from him, a hand shot out and pinched his bottom.

"You better cut that out," he said in a whisper. "If you get me started, there won't be any show tonight."

"Okay, but how about after the show?" She winked that dynamite wink and curled her tongue to her top lip. Then she moved away toward the bedroom.

Nate slumped back down onto the worn, old lavender-brown sofa, which, like all the other deteriorating furniture, had come furnished with the apartment.

Another fury avoided by quick thinking, he told himself, a flash of pride parading itself through his mind. Leaning his head back over the top of the worn couch, he felt his body instantly relax. He hadn't realized how exhausted he was until this moment. In a matter of moments, he could be sleeping, he felt certain. Maybe going to the theater tonight wasn't such a good idea, after all. No, he could sleep anytime, but he couldn't do this just anytime. It was going to be a special occasion for Nathan Tibbetts and his woman, his soon-to-be bride, Casta Jordan.

Slowly, he pushed himself upward, until he was sitting on the edge of the sofa. Then gradually, he rose to his feet. He knew that once he got himself going again, his energy would return and that he would enjoy himself. Maybe a shower would help.

He struggled into the bathroom and began to get undressed. After he finished the shower and while he was drying himself off, he called to Casta, whom he could see still thoroughly clothed in the bedroom. "Say, this soap really does make you come alive again!"

"Wrong brand, Nate," she shouted back.

"Oh, well, I guess any of 'em do, don't they?"

"It's really the water, not the soap, you know. That's just another one of their advertising gimmicks."

Bouncing, he presented his nude body before her. "Da-dum-m-m!" he said, imitating a drum roll.

"Okay, Mr. America, I see you." But she smiled anyway.

He began to check out his clothing options in the closet. "What should I — ?"

"Oh, Nate, I nearly forgot to tell you, what with your soap commercial and all."

He turned. "What?"

"I called Shirley Wynn and arranged to borrow her car for tonight. I thought it might be classier than going to the theater by bus."

"Great!"

"Only catch is that Martin and Babes got it now, but she said they should be back by seven."

"Oh, well, if they're not, I guess we could call a taxi."

"What's this? You suddenly made of money, Mr. Tibbetts? Buying tickets to the theater, taking me out to eat, and hiring a taxi all in one night. If I didn't know better, I'd think you were about to ask me the *big* question. But you already done that, so it must be something else."

"Come on, Casta. I'm not that bad."

"Okay, okay." And she kissed him again, briefly.

The telephone's ringing interrupted them, and she stood. Mischievously, her eyes glided down below his waist as she walked away. "Better put that thing down or we'll never make it to Jonah's," she said. Then she picked up the receiver. He couldn't help laughing.

"Thanks, Shirley, we really 'preciate it," he heard her say.

Casta replaced the receiver and came back toward him.

"Martin's gonna drop the car by in about ten minutes," she said. "So you won't have to do your big spender bit, after all."

They decided to go semi-formal, so he pulled his black sateen suit out of the closet. It looked nice, even if it hadn't cost much. Just as he was fumbling with his tie, he heard a knock at the door.

"Must be Martin. I'll get it," he said.

He was right. Martin held out the keys. "Have a nice time," he said, simply.

"Want to come in for a second?"

"Naw. Got to hit the books. Hope you enjoy the show. Where you going?"

"To Jonah's."

"Jonah's?"

"Yeah, it's a dinner theater."

"Oh, big time!" And Martin held both his thumbs up in front of his chest.

"Sure, sure."

"Too high falutin' to go to the movies anymore, huh?" the other added, smiling.

Nate shoved Martin into the hall and pulled the door partially closed behind them.

"It's just that I got the tickets free, that's all," he said in a near-whisper. "But don't tell Casta."

"You can count on me." And Martin winked and turned and began to walk down the stairs. "Have a good time," he repeated.

Nate was about to return to the apartment when he heard Martin call up to him. "Oh, Shirl said tell you to just keep the car overnight. She'll call ya tomorrow morning. Okay?"

"Got it," Nate shouted.

Driving over, Casta snuggled tightly against him, clutching his right upper arm with both her hands. But they rode most of the way without conversation. The trip took them down Pearl Street, then right on Second, and past St. Thaddeus. Seeing the hospital again took his mind off the evening of fun which they had in store, and he resented that. Then he felt guilty because of his resentment.

Oh. Mama. I'm sorry. But what should I do?

"What should I do, Mama?"

Almost a week had passed since they had placed Otis in the ground, and he'd hardly been out of the house.

"Anything. Just stop this here mopin' 'round. You gotta get your mind off it, Sonny."

"How, Mama? How? What can I do?"

"I ain't been seein' you readin' much lately. Why don't you go in there and read one of them comic books of yours?"

"Can't, Mama. Done tried that. I couldn't stop thinking about Otis. Anyway, most of 'em are his. *Was* his."

Mama didn't say anything for a few minutes. She continued with her cooking. Finally, she left the room. When she returned, she was holding a five-dollar bill in her hand.

"Here, Sonny. Why don't you go down to th' movies. And buy ya'self somethin' to eat 'n drank. How's that?"

Nate smiled up at her. "O-kay! Thanks, Mama."

Five minutes later he was sailing out the door.

"You want to talk about it?" he heard Casta say.

He glanced around at her warm, gentle face. But he didn't speak.

"Couldn't hurt," she continued.

"Later. Maybe later," he said, finally.

She squeezed his arm even more tightly and dropped her head onto his shoulder. It was no wonder that Mama liked Casta so much. They were so much alike. Just like Mama, she seemed to know when something was bothering him.

"It was so sweet of you to think of coming out like this. I really 'preciate it," she was saying.

"Well, I was a little selfish, too. I wanted to see the play, myself."

"Don't be too surprised if you don't enjoy it much," she said.

He looked around at her, a quizzical expression on his face. Their eyes never met, but she accurately guessed his gesture.

"It's just that it's a period piece," she continued. "It probably won't mean to us what it did to them, over a hundred years ago."

"Oh, well, maybe."

"But that's fine by me. And don't worry about it. I'm going to have a great time." She ran the fingers of her right hand across his cheek. "This is going to be a special evening I'm going to remember forever."

There was parking adjacent to the theater and even a parking lot attendant. Arm-in-arm, the two of them strolled into the foyer and Nate presented the tickets.

"This way, sir," the smiling host said, escorting them to a table with a splendid view of the stage.

As Casta had predicted, he found the show rather dated, and he had trouble keeping his mind on the performance. At the conclusion, however, he smiled and applauded hardily, as did most of the others attending.

"Thanks, Tib. It was much better than I expected. Really very good for something that old. I thought it would be more out-of-date," Casta told him, smiling broadly. He couldn't tell if she was simply trying to show her appreciation or if she really had enjoyed the play that much. But he decided to play along.

"You know, once you become Mrs. Tibbetts — oops, I forgot, you're not gonna change your name — but, once we're joined in *holy wedlock*" — he winked at her — "then we'll do this kinda thing all the time."

"Anything you say." And Nate realized that even wearing a smirk Casta was a striking beauty.

They were still sitting, staring at each other-across the table when Nate discovered that the theater was practically empty.

"Hey, we better get outa here before they throw us out," he said, grinning broadly and taking her hand as he stood.

The host held the door for them, but, as they approached the exit, Nate experienced an odd reluctance to leave the theater. He released his grip on Casta's hand and rubbed his right temple, trying to bring his thoughts into sharper focus. By the time they actually reached the exit, Casta was already a half-dozen feet ahead of him, and Nate slowed up even more, for there was something strange and indefinable inside his mind, and he felt a desperate need to sort it out.

Just at the doorway, he paused, and, a split-second later, he felt a hand encircle his arm. Then he stood and watched it — the most terrible sight his eyes could ever behold.

There was Casta, now more than a dozen feet ahead, taking each step in very slow, extremely well-defined measures. But there was other movement near her. Above her head. Traveling much more rapidly than Casta. Downward. On a collision course with her beautiful body.

Nate tried to scream, but he couldn't. All sound seemed locked inside his throat, and he couldn't get it to pass outward. His eyes were stretched wide in disbelief as he watched the theater's heavy metal awning come crashing down first on Casta's head, then onto her shoulders. As she crumpled downward under the tremendous weight, she still didn't seem to be moving quite rapidly enough. The whole scene appeared drawn-out, distorted, and grotesque in Nate's eyes. And all the while, he continued to experience a series of blurred images inside his head.

The grip around his upper arm tightened, constricting his circulation, but bringing a sense of reality to what otherwise almost seemed a fantasy vision. He glanced around and saw the host clutching him in an iron grasp and also the horror in the other man's eyes, and Nate knew that this was no fantasy. It was all real — very real.

He felt his lungs released also, and he stared toward the mangled wreckage of metal and flesh and bellowed, "Watch out!"

Too late! Too late! Much too late. His life — his whole life — lay but a few feet away, crushed and bleeding. His whole reason for existing lay silent in a silence he knew would never be broken, yet he felt his sense of loss begin to slip away — into a back corner of his mind. Instead, he was suddenly gripped by an overwhelming fear. Something in those weird images — those distorted thoughts — made his mind flash back over the last four days of his life.

First, there had been the partially severed rope. Then, the two thugs in the alley.

And now this!

A horrifying conviction ripped through his mind: *Someone was trying very hard to kill him!*

INTERLUDE D

"I'm sorry, Cougar, to disturb you like this — "

"It better be important. What is it?"

"I'm afraid my men got the wrong one. They killed the girl."

"Again! Failure on their part is becoming a pattern, Panther. We can't afford another slipshod operation like Guantanamo or that fiasco during the Presidential primaries. This has to be a clean affair, so I suggest you take measures immediately. Perhaps you need some fresh blood — a change in manpower."

"Sir, I don't believe that's necessary at this point, but I would like to make a change in procedure. If you remember — "

"I do, Panther, go on."

"Yes, sir. Well, then, if you examine closely the latest graphs I sent you, you will find that his pattern is quite different from all the other first-generation descendants of Gamov's experiments. There can be no doubt about the permanent alteration of his gene chain. And the longer this drags on, the more apparent those differences become."

"Then I suggest you proceed with haste, man."

"Yes, sir. But I feel that if we continue with the present procedure, we can only end up with more failures."

"Why? Do you think he realizes what's happening to him?"

"*I'm not certain.*"

"*Then what are you suggesting, Panther?*"

"*I believe we need more direct study. If he really is that* different, *then perhaps we should employ a* different approach.*"

"*How do you propose going about this? Do you plan more*
first-person contact?*"

"*No, not myself, not at this point. But I do feel we should make contact, to get some answers. Perhaps, then, we'll be prepared to mount a new, more successful procedure.*"

"*All right, Panther, I'll approve this. But don't take too long. If things are as serious as you suggest, we may not have much time.*"

CHAPTER EIGHT

The whole thing had taken less than two seconds, yet Nate knew it really must have been eons.

Over and over, the scene ran through his mind. If he had only been beside her, perhaps he could have pushed her safely beyond the falling death, perhaps he could have saved them both. Or would the awning simply have crushed him, too, before he could act? He wanted to believe that. It would help relieve the guilt if he only could, but he couldn't. Still, something had caused him to hold back, something had made him let Casta step under that awning alone. What? What was it? He tried to focus on what had flashed through his head only split-seconds before it had occurred, but he couldn't bring it to the front. It had been too nebulous, anyway. It never had been a clearly definable thought.

Silently, he stood there staring at her crushed body, now free of the heavy awning. Less than a minute after what he knew was a murder attempt, he had joined with the theater host and passersby and others from the show to lift the heavy metal and pull Casta free. But he had known that it was no use. He was certain that no life remained inside her shattered body. And he'd been right.

In the distance, Nate could hear the wail of the ambulance siren, coming on a fruitless mission. But his mind had already begun to drift in other directions as

the vehicle came screeching to a halt just a few feet
away.

The cut rope.

The two thugs.

The murdered lover.

Why? Why? What did it mean? Why was someone
trying to kill him? What did he have that could possibly
cause someone to want to kill him? Or maybe it was
something he had done. But what?

Oh, sure he'd had his share of skirmishes, but
there'd never been anything to drive someone to such
methodical mayhem. Or had there? And who? Who
could be behind it?

When the rope had broken, he'd been out with Casta
and Babes, Martin and Shirley. Then, Alland had given
him the tickets. But Casta had sent him for spaghetti —
spaghetti she should have purchased herself. Finally,
he'd been out with Casta, and she'd gotten killed. The
only unifying factor was Casta. She was involved in it
all. Nate found a grisly thought passing through his
mind, and he tried desperately to push it aside, but it
wouldn't budge.

Casta! Had she been trying to kill him for some mad
reason and gotten caught up in her own plot? No, it
didn't make sense. And even if that was the case, she
had had accomplices.

He tried to erase these thoughts and start over, to try
and come up with something sensible, but they kept
coming back, kept plaguing him. Finally, he was pulled
back to reality by a man dressed in a navy blue
uniform.

"Sir, were you with the victim when the accident
occurred?" the policeman was asking.

Victim? The cop had said "victim!" Even he knew it
wasn't really an accident.

"Uh, yes, I was," he found himself responding.

"You had been to the theater and were leaving?"

"Yes. You see Casta and I lived toget — that it, we were engaged. We were to be married next month."

"I see. Your name?"

"Pardon?"

"What is your name, sir?"

"Tibbetts. Nathan Tibbetts."

"Thank you, Mr. Tibbetts. I'm going to have to ask you to remain here for a few more moments, until Lieutenant Corley can take your statement."

Nate glanced over and saw the ambulance crew loading the covered body of Casta Jordan into the back of the ambulance. The policeman followed his eyes, and, when the vehicle's rear door slammed shut, he resumed speaking.

"I'm sorry, Mr. Tibbetts," he said softly.

Nate nodded, but he did not look around at the man.

Momentarily, he heard the other walk away.

Long after the ambulance had disappeared from view, he continued to stare after it. When he heard someone approaching him, he presumed it was the police lieutenant, so he broke his gaze and turned his head slightly.

But it was the theater host. "I really don't know how to begin this, young man...but I felt I must try. You must understand nothing like this has ever happened here before. We've always maintained this building so well I don't understand how it could have happened...."

Bastard! He wasn't trying to say he was sorry that Casta was dead. He was trying to defend the damn theater's reputation. What the hell did he care about this place? The son-of-a-bitch was making him sick. He felt like turning around and slugging the guy.

But he didn't. Instead, he held up a hand, interrupting the babbler. "I understand. It was an accident, that's all" — like hell it was, but he couldn't afford to play his hand with anyone; he just didn't know whom to trust — "and it could have happened anywhere.... Thank you."

Nate held out his hand to the boot-licker. It seemed like the quickest way to get rid of him. The other took it and shook it vigorously. But he didn't leave. He resumed his repetitious babble.

Out of the corner of his eyes, Nate saw another man making his way toward them, and he felt a dryness in his mouth. The man was tall, maybe six-four or six-five, and Nate's mind flashed back to the previous evening and a dark alley and a tall man with a knife. He tried to pull his hand free of the other man's grip, but the host wouldn't release him.

Now, Nate was staring directly toward the tall man who was quickly closing the gap between them. God, here he was being held captive by a babbling idiot while a murderer stalked him. He jerked his hand hard, and the other let go of it reluctantly, although he didn't stop talking.

Christ, the man surely wasn't going to try to finish him off right in front of all these witnesses. But he was still closing.

Run! He had to escape. "They" — whoever "they" were — must be getting desperate now. They might try anything.

But why? Why did they want him dead?

He swung around, seeking the best avenue of escape, and was about to put his feet in gear.

"Wait. Don't move, Tibbetts."

And they froze. No matter now hard he tried, he couldn't get them to move.

Here was a murderer closing in on him, and he couldn't even flee. Why? So many "why's"! But this one he understood. He knew why he wasn't running: Answers. He wanted answers. And this guy might give them to him.

But, no! It was the other who demanded answers of Nate. About five feet away, he halted and put his hand inside his coat —

God, he's going for a gun! He's going to shoot me down right here!

— and pulled out a police badge.

"I'm Lieutenant Corley. I wonder if I could ask you a few questions."

A cop! This was the lieutenant the uniformed officer had referred to a few moments ago. But, for some reason, Nate had been expecting another uniformed policeman.

Nate exhaled slightly. "Certainly, lieutenant."

"Mr. Tibbetts, I know this must be painful for you, so I will try to keep my questions brief."

"Thank you, I — " Suddenly, Nate felt an image flashing through his mind. He knew it was the same image he'd seen right before Casta had been killed, and, had he been able to fully concentrate on it, he might have been able to draw it fully into focus. But he couldn't. The lieutenant was speaking again, and the image once more began to fade.

"I understand you were with" — Corley held up a driver's license and examined it for a second — "Miss Jordan at the time of her death. Is that right?

"Yes."

"And you were coming out of the theater here?" He pointed toward the front door of Jonah's.

Nate nodded.

"Would you tell me what happened?"

Nate cupped his chin in his left hand and stared at the mass of twisted metal nearby. "As you've said, we were leaving when it happened — when the roof fell on her."

"Yes, I see. Where were you when it happened — in

relation to Miss Jordan, I mean."

Again Nate nodded. "Oh, that. I was behind her...several feet..."

"That's right, officer," the theater host said, interrupting.

"He was standing beside me when the awning fell in. The young lady had gone ahead."

"Why?" The question was clearly directed at Nate. "Sir?"

"Why was the lady several feet ahead of you."

The image flashed through his mind again, but too quickly for him to pin it down.

"I, uh... I don't...know." Nate said, shrugging.

"Officer..." The theater host was speaking again. Corley shifted his gaze to take in the middle-aged, pudgy attendant. "Officer, I stopped him. I saw the awning caving in, and I reached out and grabbed this young man's arm."

"Yes" — nodding — "he did, lieutenant." Only, Nate remembered slowing down before he felt the hand encircle his arm.

"Oh, I see." Corley closed a small, spiral pad he'd been writing in and pocketed it. "Then I don't believe I have any further questions. You're free to go now, Mr. Tibbetts. Thank you, and I'm very sorry."

The policeman took a step toward the other man. "I wonder if I could ask you a few more questions..." Nate heard Corley say as he began to move away from the others.

He stumbled toward the parking lot, which he found practically empty and unattended. Slipping into Shirley's little red Toyota, he suddenly was overwhelmed with the dreamlike quality of what he'd just been through. He dropped his head back and closed his eyes, trying to believe that when he opened them he would see Cass sitting beside him, laughing. But it didn't happen. Instead, what he saw again was that slow-motion scene of the theater roof crashing in on Casta. And then her lovely body lying there on the cold concrete, lying there crushed and bleeding.

Once again, he felt a conviction that the events of the past four days had not been strictly happenstance. Someone out there was trying to murder him, and he had not the slightest inkling why. A feeling of frustration gripped him also, for without an understanding of why this was happening, he had no idea how he could protect himself from another assault. And another assault there must certainly be — for whoever was doing this surely wouldn't give up now. If he, she, or they had gone through all this, there was no reason to think it would stop.

His theory about Casta's connection with the incidence flashed through his mind again, but once more he pushed it aside. Wasn't it bad enough that she was gone without him having to crucify her in his thoughts?

But what am I supposed to do?

The drive home was a surrealistic nightmare. Nate kept getting strange thoughts and memories which he couldn't account for.

He seriously began to question his own sanity.

His mind raced again and again over Casta's death, over his hesitation, and the theater host's grip on his arm. Suddenly, he was seeing the whole scene from a different perspective: Maybe a hundred yards away and some distance off the ground. Then, he had the sensation of standing atop the theater building itself and of releasing something which had held the awning up.

No. no! Nate told himself. This couldn't be happening. But he knew that he had at last recaptured the image he'd felt just before Casta's death. And the reason he hadn't been able to sort it out before was because it was not one but two images blurred together. Still, somehow, his mind had understood the image enough to make him hesitate. That was it! He knew it was. He wasn't insane. Somehow, he had felt as though he were standing in three places all at once in that instant right before the roof came crashing down on Casta.

But still, it made no sense. Or did it?

Swinging right on Pearl Street, he felt a new image enter his mind. He had the impression that he was riding along behind a red Toyota — the one he was *driving* — and watching it closely. He glanced up into the rear-view mirror just in time to see the lights of another vehicle swinging left off Second onto Pearl right behind him.

My god! "They" were following him! Or were they? Was he letting his mind play tricks on him in his state of heightened anxiety? He wanted to believe that, but he had to be sure. He shoved the accelerator to the floor, and the little car moved away from the rest of the traffic. The car behind him speeded up too. He pulled into the extreme right lane, and the other car pulled over also. He slowed up, and the other vehicle slowed at the same rate, making no effort to pass.

Yes, they were definitely following him.

He pushed the accelerator down again, charging away, with some vague thought of trying to outrun his pursuers, but he soon abandoned that idea. No, obviously, whoever this was knew too much about him. Even if he lost his "tail," they would simply circle back to his apartment and wait for him to return. Then What?

Answers. He still wanted answers. Maybe he should just play along for right now. Just drive back to his place and see what happened. Therefore, at a moderate speed, he proceeded to do just that.

Nate parked Shirley's car in the closest parking space he could find to his apartment, almost a block away. He watched as the pursuit vehicle shot past him, then pulled into a parking space nearby. Either the jerk driving that car didn't know much about following people or he wanted Nate to realize he was there. Nate didn't know which, but he couldn't risk letting the other find that he was conscious of his presence. So he slipped out and walked briskly toward his apartment building without looking in the direction of the other vehicle.

Once inside his building, he practically flew up the stairs to the second floor. He jerked out his key, quickly unlocking his door and slipping inside. Moving over to the living room window, he pulled the shade back very slightly in order to get a view of the other car and its occupants. He had only glanced it peripherially as it passed him, realizing it was a cream color, but not how many people were inside. Now, his eyes swept along the street to the space where the car had parked, and he found it — empty! The car was gone!

He let the shade fall back into place.

The dryness in his throat was back, and he rubbed the palms of his hands together and blew into them, despite the more than 80-degree temperature.

As he made his way back over to his apartment door to lock it, he found himself wishing the cream-colored car were still parked outside his apartment. At least, there, he could keep an eye on it.

CHAPTER NINE

He ached.

There was a throbbing which seemed to be coming from every muscle of his body. In fact, just getting from the door to the sofa had been a chore. His body felt like it had gained a hundred pounds in the last ten seconds.

Rest. He had to rest. He knew it must be late, but he didn't have the strength to even lift his wrist and look at his watch.

Nate dropped his head onto the top of the sofa and closed his eyes.

Sleep. Sweet sleep.

But sleep wouldn't grace him with its presence. His mind was still spinning with all kinds of pictures and images. Some were real, he knew, for he had experienced them. But others were there, too. Others that had an elusive quality of reality mixed with fantasy. Many of the images seemed real in the sense that he could focus on details, but he knew they couldn't be real because he had never actually experienced these things.

Slowly, with more effort than he'd thought he could expend, he raised a hand and rubbed his forehead. Dizzy, so dizzy. Maybe his mind was slipping.

"No!" he shouted, jerking his eyes open angrily. He wouldn't have it. He *wasn't* going crazy.

Tired. So tired. All he really needed was rest. He

would get up and go to bed if he only had the energy.

But he couldn't sleep. Not now. He didn't know what it all meant. He had to figure it out. To put the pieces together.

The scenes of the last few days began to run through his mind again in rapid-fire action, and he felt powerless to control his thoughts. Again and again, they zipped by; however, they still made no sense.

A puzzle! That's what he was seeing in his mind. The pieces of a giant, living jigsaw puzzle. But they didn't fit. The pieces didn't fit. Then maybe it wasn't a puzzle...

Oh, yes it was. That's exactly what it was. A jigsaw puzzle. But the reason he couldn't get the pieces to fit together was because some of the pieces were missing. Some of the *most vital pieces*, were missing. He couldn't solve this puzzle until he found the missing pieces.

Suddenly, he remembered the cream-colored car, and he knew he had to find the pieces soon. Because, if he didn't, the pieces might come together in his own destruction. And he could not, he must not, let that happen.

Nate slowly opened his eyes again, his mind clearing, the exhaustion mysteriously dissipating. He looked around the room, realizing the agony wasn't over — that it was just about to take a new form.

His fingers made their way across the fabric of the worn couch. The same couch on which he'd sat only a few hours ago hugging a young woman named Casta Jordan. The same Casta Jordan who only a short time after that became a non-entity, nothing but a mangled piece of flesh. Slowly, he ran his fingers in and out of the grooves in the fabric material, and he suddenly realized that he couldn't sit here, not tonight.

Springing to his feet with an agility which only a few seconds before had not existed within his body, he could not stop his eyes from roaming about the room, taking in the bookcase, with the framed picture standing atop it, a picture of two people smiling. One was pale of complexion, while the other, a woman, was a creamy chocolate color. They both seemed so content, so happy to be together. But they had no right to smile now, Nate knew. They were mocking him. With an effort, he shifted his gaze, taking in a stack of sewing, piled uncompleted in one corner of the room. Needlework, she'd called it, and it had belonged to that same woman, to that same non-entity, in the photograph.

No more! He couldn't take any more. He squeezed his eyes together tightly and started to slump backwards onto the sofa once more. But he caught himself, stumbled, hit his knee on the coffee table, regained his balance, and struggled over to "his" chair.

However, "his" chair was no better. It afforded him too good a view of "her" kitchen.

Oh, Christ, he couldn't take this. He was going mad. He knew he was going mad.

Sleep, yes, sleep. Now, he remembered how tired he had felt a few moments before. Sleep was the ticket. It would clear his groggy mind. And now maybe he had the strength to make it to the bedroom.

He did. But it didn't help. He lay on "his" side of the double bed thinking, still thinking. Somehow, he had to turn off his mind and rest. But how could he sleep here in the bed where he'd shared so many joyous moments of love with "her"?

Finally, he staggered to his feet and went into the toilet to relieve himself.

Oh, God, even the bathroom held memories.

But what was he supposed to do?

"Casta! Casta, Casta, Casta, please come back. I'll follow all your advice. I'll do whatever you want me to. Promise. Just don't leave me, now. Please, Cass, don't."

He realized suddenly that he had been screaming the words as loud as he possibly could, but he didn't care. "No, Casta. God, no! No, no, no! Dammit, woman, why don't you ever do what I say?"

Then, he heard a voice — a very reassuring voice. But the voice was inside his head, and it was reaching across time. He could hear Mama talking to him, and he could picture her image with crystal clarity as she said: "We can mourn 'em, but we can't bring 'em back."

"No, Mama, you're wrong!" he shouted, holding up both his hands to her phantom image as he struggled back into the bedroom. "You're wrong, this time. You've got to be wrong."

"...we can't bring 'em back..."

He covered his ears with his hands, but Mama's voice didn't stop.

"...we can't...we can't!...we can't!...we can't!..."

"Stop it, Mama! Stop it."

"...we can't bring 'em back..."

His eyes drifted around the bedroom, but the phantom image of his mother, as well as the room's contents became obscured by the well of salty water surrounding his eyes. This place wasn't much, though it had been theirs. *Theirs!* And now it never could be again.

"Please, Casta," he pleaded. "Please come back!" Sobbing, he fell to his bees beside the bed which the two of them had shared. "What more do you want of me, woman? I love you. Don't you know that? I love you. No! God, no! I *loved* you." And now it was over. Forever!

His head fell onto the bed and his fountain of tears drenched the covers.

In his mind, he could see Mama again, and he remembered what else she had said after Otis' death. "We Jus' has to go on livin' ourselves."

He raised his head and sniffed. "We can mourn 'em,

but we can't ever bring 'em back... We just has to go on livin' ourselves."

Slowly, he rose to his feet again, wiping the last of the tears away with the fingers of his right hand.

Okay. Mama. It's just you and me again! But not for long, he knew.

"...go on livin'..."

And that, in itself, might be a problem. But he had to try, didn't he?

With a feel of determination in his step, he returned to the living room and pulled back the shade. That parking space was filled once more, but not with the cream-colored car. Scanning every vehicle visible to him, he soon determined that there was no cream car parked anywhere in his line of vision. Not one!

Nate let the shade drop back into place, his jaw set, his mind fixed.

"You bastards, I'll get you for this!" he mumbled, holding up a single, clenched fist and shaking it in the direction of the window. "Whatever it takes, I'll get you. For Casta Jordan — for Casta, I'll get you. By dammit, I'll find those missing pieces and figure it out."

There was a lump the size of a baseball in his throat. He tried to swallow it, but couldn't.

How? How was he going to figure it out? He had no idea whom he was fighting or why. And "they" knew all about him. In fact, what were they waiting for? Why didn't they just come charging in and shoot him down?

Almost without realizing what he was doing, he moved back over to his door and checked the lock. Yep, secure. Secure, hell! Did he seriously believe that these people would be deterred by a little thing like an apartment burglar lock? No! No chance.

Christ, he couldn't stay here just waiting around for them to call. He had to do something. He had to...

...have help! Of course, he needed help. What chance

did he have to defeat them acting alone? But who? Who could he turn to?

He didn't have to think long. He picked up the phone and started dialing.

"Huh...what? Yeah?" he heard the voice on the other end of the line say.

"Babes? It's Nate."

"'Low, Nate. Say, what time is it?"

Nate glanced down at his watch. After 3. "I'm sorry if I woke you, Babes, but I need your help — *bad!*"

Suddenly all the grogginess was gone out of his friend's voice. "What is it, Nate? You have a wreck or something? You okay?"

"No, I didn't have a wreck — but, *no,* I'm not okay. Casta's dead."

"My God!" There was a second of silence, then Babes continued. "What happened?"

"At the theater, somebody killed her, and they're after me too."

There was no comment from the other end of the line. "Babes? You still there?"

"Uh, yeah, Nate, I'm...but, shit! Somebody's trying to kill you? How? Why?"

"I don't know the answer to either."

"But, Cassie? They killed her?"

"Yes."

"What happened?"

"The theater roof — uh, awning — fell on her as we were leaving the show."

"But I thought you said — "

"I did! It *wasn't* an accident. Somebody dropped it deliberately. Only they were trying to get me, and they got her by mistake."

"But — "

"Dammit, man, it's true."

"Yeah, I know, Nate. But what makes you think it

was deliberate?"

Why did he think that? No, he *knew* it? But how did he know it?

"I just know, Babes, that's all. I *know!*"

"Okay, man."

"Babes, you've got to believe me."

"I believe you, Nate...buddy. Just hang on, okay. Things'll look better in the morning. Say, why don't you come over here for the night — for what's left of it — and stay with me? I'll put on some coffee, and we can talk this over all you want. Okay? See you in a little while?"

Nate thought for a few seconds. It was no wonder Babes didn't believe him. He sounded as though he was babbling out of control, and he really had no proof to back up his beliefs.

He tried to sound more in command of himself than he felt. "No, I'm alright now, Babes. Thanks for talking to me. I got myself together. I just needed somebody to talk to."

"Sure, Nate. But you sure you're okay, now?"

"Fine. I just been thinking about Cass, that's all. I guess it's been gettin' to me."

"You sure you don't want to come over? The invitation's still open. Or I can come over there...."

"That's alright. Sorry I woke you. Go back to sleep. 'Bye, Babes."

"Yeah. 'bye."

Slowly, Nate replaced the receiver. He'd certainly botched that one up. Now what? And maybe Babes was right. Maybe the whole thing was the distortion of a distraught mind. It could all be coincidence. But what about the car? The cream-colored job? Yeah, that too. That could be coincidence, also. Or he could have imagined that it was following him, like he had imagined those images. No! Hell no! He hadn't imagined any of it. It was real! It was too real. There was someone or someones out there trying to kill him for some unknown reason, and he was back to square one. He still needed help.

Should he try to call Babes again and try to explain what he'd meant? No, that wasn't any good. Besides, what could Babes do that he couldn't do? What he needed was some real help like...

...Like the cops! They must be used to strange stories...and to picking the truth out of improbable accounts. Surely, when they heard about all that had happened to him recently, they would see that Casta's death had been no accident. He would make them see it.

Slowly, cautiously, Nate reached for the receiver again. This time he would be cool. He would keep himself under control. He couldn't chance losing them as he'd lost Babes.

"Police. This is Officer Schmitz. Can I help you?" A pleasant enough voice. A voice under control. The kind of voice Nate would have when he spoke.

But his emotions betrayed him. "Hello...hello! This is, uh, uh... Could I please speak to, uh, Lieutenant Corley, please?"

"Certainly. One moment please." Still cool. Unshaken.

"Homicide." It was a new voice. But the man had said, "homocide." Then, they knew it was murder already. Or did they?

"Lieutenant Corley?"

"Hold on."

Nate held. About a minute later, the "homicide" voice came back on the line. "Bill's away from his desk right now. Could I be of service?"

Could he? He had to talk to someone. Why Corley? He'd just made the initial investigation. Anyone else should be just as good.

"Yes...yes, sir. I think someone's trying to, uh, kill me!" Control. He had to get his control back.

"Is it someone in the room or house where you are now?"

"No, I don't think so."

"Good. Then give me your name and address, please."

"Nathan Tibbetts, 716 Pearl, Apt. 2C."

"Okay, Mr. Tibbetts, you say someone is trying to kill you. Who is it and what makes you think this?"

As calmly as he could, Nate told the officer about Casta's death at the theater and about the other events during the past four — no, now it had been five — days.

"I see," the officer replied when he'd finished, and Nate was certain he had created another non-believer. "And where are you now, Mr. Tibbetts?"

"At my apartment."

"Good. Why don't you just stay put there for a while, and I'll have Bill get back to you when he comes in, alright?"

"Uh, yeah, that's fine."

"Your number please?"

"...Number?"

"Yeah, sure...your telephone number?"

"Oh, that number. It's 848-1764."

"...7-6-4. Got it. I'll have Bill contact you. Don't forget, just stay put."

"Yes, sir."

Nate continued to hold the receiver to his ear for several seconds after he heard the click on the other end of the line.

Would he really tell Lieutenant Corley to call back? Or was this guy just humoring him? No, he would. He'd been very emphatic that Nate should stick around and wait for Corley to call back. Anyway, where would he go at 3 o'clock in the morning?

Moving back over to the window, he checked for the

cream-colored car again. Way down the street, he could see a vehicle which might be cream-colored, but he couldn't be sure by the meager light from the street lamp. He squinted and pressed his face tightly against the glass to try and get a better view. Was it cream or wasn't it? For that matter, even if it was, that didn't mean it was the car that had followed him. But it might be!

He stood at the window for several minutes, alternating pressing his face against it and squinting at the car.

Then he caught himself. Christ, what a dummy he was. Suppose "they" were standing somewhere out there watching him. Watching him, aiming a high-powered rifle at his head.

His eyes zipped about the street below as he removed his face from the window and smoothed the shade back into place against it.

Whew!

Now, Nate began to back away from the window on tiptoes. Backing, backing until his hand brushed against "his" chair. Suddenly, he grabbed it and dragged it around so that it faced toward the window, then he dropped into it.

Come on, Corley. Call! Call, dammit!

He felt a cramping in the pit of his stomach, and he wondered if he was going to lose his dinner. That delicious steak that he and...and — shit! Goddamn, Jonah's! If he hadn't taken her there tonight, she would still be alive. And if he hadn't fought with her and insisted on going to class, he might not have felt obligated to take her out. They could have stayed home and enjoyed themselves. Oh, shit, what a thought. He was thinking about sex, and Casta only dead a few hours. What kind of pervert was he?

There was moisture on Nate's cheeks, and his hand

went up to brush the tears away.

"Dammit! Why couldn't — ?"

What was that? A noise. He knew he'd heard a noise. Outside his apartment. Or was it inside?

Holding his breath, he inched his hands out to the arms of his chair and pushed himself to a standing position.

Listening.

No. Nothing.

Wait! There it was again!

A kind of creaking.

Outside.

It was outside in the hallway.

Someone was outside in the hallway.

At this hour? He let himself glance quickly at his watch again. Almost four o'clock. There shouldn't be anyone out there at this time of the morning.

But he could hear the creaking. It was getting louder. Whoever it was was coming for him!

"Oh, shit, no!" he mumbled under his breath.

Glancing around the room with a vague thought of finding a hiding place, his eyes snared the phone. That was it! He'd call the police again.

No. No good. They couldn't get here in time. And besides, whoever that was out there might hear him.

The sound was unmistakable now. It was the sound of footfalls.

Then...

Knock.

Knock.

Knock.

Nate stood frozen, not moving, not breathing.

Again...

Knock.

Knock.

Where could he hide?

Where that they wouldn't find him? Nowhere! There

was no place to hide in this tiny apartment.

Once more...

Knock.

And...

(Louder) Knock, knock.

Christ, why? Why would they be knocking on his door if — ?

"Hello in there. This is the police. Would you mind opening the door?"

The cops! Thank God!

He fumbled with the lock for what seemed like hours before he got it unfastened.

Then he jerked the door open, and there stood —

— Not Corley!

Christ, it was the oldest trick in the world, and he'd fallen for it.

But the man was smiling, and he was holding something out toward Nate. It was a *police badge.*

Nate realized now that the man was speaking, and he tried to tune in the words.

"...involved on another case, and he asked me to come down. May I come in, Mr. Tibbetts?"

"Huh? I...yeah! Come in."

Nate stood back out of the way to let the pale, blue-eyed cop enter. As he passed through the doorway, Nate noticed the other's height. Damn, was everyone else in the world six-and-half feet tall?

The man was holding out a hand. "I'm Sergeant Lacy...Julian Lacy."

"Oh, yes. Yes, sir." He took Lacy's hand, trying to offer a firm grip, and shook it. He cleared his throat, attempting to bring his heartbeat down to normal before he continued.

The sergeant released his hand and glanced around the apartment.

Sweat was dripping off Nate's brow, but he tried to

look as if he were under control as he stared at Lacy's face.

"Thank you, uh, sergeant, for coming over. Won't you have a seat?"

Lacy nodded and backed over to the sofa, lowering himself. Nate stood for a second longer as his breathing slowed, then he dropped down into his chair.

"Now, Mr. Tibbetts, I understand that you fear for your safety. Is that correct?"

"Uh, yeah. Yes!" Nate replied, nodding.

"Would you mind telling me about it?"

Nate tried to smile as he pitched into the account as he'd given it to the other policeman on the phone a short time before.

"There is one thing I'm not sure I understand," Lacy said when he had finished. "Why were you so far behind Miss Jordan when the two of you were leaving the theater?"

"Uh, well, the theater doorman grabbed me when he saw the roof about to cave in." Why didn't he tell him the rest? No, that could ruin it. He had to stick to the "facts" — the cold facts. Police didn't like to hear about "visions."

"But Miss Jordan was already several feet ahead of you by this time. Isn't that right?"

"Some. She was ahead of me some. Just a few feet, I guess."

"Why was that?"

Christ! Did this guy suspect he had something to do with Casta's death.

"Uh, well, I...I don't know. Maybe it was just because we were going through the door and I was acting like...I was trying to be a gentleman, by letting her go first. I haven't really thought about it much."

Liar!

Had he thought that?

"I, uh, beg your pardon?"

Lacy shook his head. "I didn't say anything."

"Oh."

There was a pause in the discussion while Lacy's eyes wandered around the room again.

"I understand that you and Miss Jordan were engaged?" the policeman said, finally.

"Yes, that's right." Now what was he after? Maybe asking the cops for help was the wrong thing, after all.

Lacy's eyes met his again. "But I gather that you two also lived together. Is that correct?"

Hell, it didn't take a Sherlock Holmes to deduce that. Nate nodded. "For almost a year."

"And you were to be married..."

"In June. Next month, when I graduate. We're going — that is, we were going — to get married on June 19.

"I see."

Nate cleared his throat.

"You're a fairly young man to be graduating from college, aren't you? I understand you're not yet 20."

"My birthday's week-after-next." But how did Lacy know his age? Had he been checking up on him?

Lacy began to rise. "Splendid achievement. Finishing college at 20."

"Thank you." Nate rose also.

"We'll check out your theory that someone tampered with the awning at Jonah's. If there was such tampering, there should be evidence. A thing like that is pretty hard to hide. That is, I imagine it is."

Lacy took a step away from the sofa toward Nate. "But I think we should definitely go on the assumption that you are right until we know otherwise. Perhaps you better come with me so we can find a place of safety for you."

Damn! So Lacy did believe him, after all. At least, this cop didn't think he was a raving lunatic.

"What about clothes? Should I pack — "

"No, never mind that. Let's just get going right away. We'll send someone down later to pick up your things for you."

"Whatever you say."

Lacy was leading the way to the door when the phone rang. Nate glanced at the policeman, who was standing frozen in his tracks, then he moved over to answer it. Out of the corners of his eyes, he saw the other man shake his head slightly as he reached for the receiver. And, as he raised the instrument to his ear, Nate noticed the bulge just at the other man's waist and the hand darting inside the coat toward that bulge.

CHAPTER TEN

With one gigantic yank, he ripped the phone cord from the wall and turned to face Lacy.

Nate could see a hand pulling a revolver up, up, up. But it seemed to be moving in slow motion just as he had perceived the crashing of the awning which killed Casta. He had plenty of time to aim his weapon and hurl it toward its target. The phone box had already struck Lacy squarely on the forehead before the other could even bring his pistol into position.

Watching, Nate felt again as though he had drifted into some fantasy world. He saw Lacy release his grip on the weapon, and it begin its slow movement toward the apartment floor. He glanced up and observed the agony on the other man's face and that Lacy was now arched backwards in the first stages of a fall. Dropping his focus, Nate discovered that the gun still had more than a foot to go before it hit the floor. Lacy's knees bent sharply and his body was thrown back almost parallel to the floor. The gun was just making contact with the carpet as Lacy's feet shot upward and his entire body began floating downward. The back of the man's head made contact with the edge of the coffee table, twisting him sideways and changing the entire angle of his fall. His knees touched the carpeting at the exact instant the fingers of his right hand also did. Then, Lacy's body obscured that hand as it passed into Nate's line of vision; however, it sprang back up an inch or two, and Lacy rolled over onto his face.

Abruptly, everything returned to its normal speed.

Nate opened his mouth wide, sucking at air, feeling as though he was about to suffocate. His right hand went up to his chest, but he found it rising and falling even more swiftly than usual. Glancing down at the man lying at his feet, he saw that Lacy's chest was also moving rhythmically.

With the realization that he hadn't killed the other man, Nate found his feet freed from their prison. He stumbled toward Lacy — and past him. He found the door unlocked and jerked it open. Now, he realized that he could not only walk but run as well, so he sent himself flying out of the apartment. When he hit the sidewalk in front of his apartment building, he did not even slow up. Wildly, he charged — past the alley where he'd been beaten up, past Crystal Street, past Market, and Second. And onward he ran. Finally, he swung right onto Sixth.

At last he slowed. And listened. Listened for the sound of feet running in pursuit. Nothing. All was quiet.

Finally, he ducked into a recessed storefront and slumped downward against the brick wall.
Now what?

He certainly couldn't go back to his apartment. Not tonight. Not as long as "they" were after him. Surely — whoever "they" were — they would watch it closely.

But what about Shirley's car? Should he risk going back for it? No, they knew it, too.

Dammit, he felt like kicking himself for not hopping into it the instant he came out of the apartment. That would have been the time to go for the car. It would've caught anyone who was working with Lacy — or whatever his name was — off guard. But now it was too late for that. For all he knew, Lacy himself might be on his trail by now, though he didn't see how, after the wallop the man had taken. The image of Lacy crashing to the floor came back to mind, and he saw the whole scene over in minute detail. But how? What was wrong with him that caused him to see things like that and to see "visions"? Had his mind completely snapped? Was he too far gone for help?

No, he couldn't believe that. There had to be some other explanation. But what? What the hell was wrong with him?

And Lacy — what if he really was a cop like he'd said? Nate could think of only two possible answers to that question. Perhaps he was just what he indicated he was, a cop investigating Nate's story, a cop who was about to take him into protective custody. Then, why the gun? Why had he been pulling out his revolver when Nate slugged him with the phone? No, that seemed unlikely. But there was always another possibility. He could be a cop who was mixed up in this effort to kill him. That made sense — of a sort. He certainly knew about Nate's contacting the authorities. In either event, all cops were off limits until this puzzle was pieced together.

But all that brought him back to "now what?" again.

He had no answers and very little idea where to start. And...

No transportation.

No place to stay.

And very little money on his person.

However, he had to have all of these before long if he hoped to survive even long enough to start checking things out.

Twice before in the last hour or so he'd turned to others for help, and both times he'd failed. But he-knew he had no choice but to try again. Now, he needed help more than before.

Who could he turn to this time? Not any of his friends at Wehling. "They" would surely be watching them closely. But it had to be someone whom he knew he could trust.

"Kidder!" Of course, Kidder McBride. In junior high and high school, they had been almost inseparable. But Kidder had gotten Clarice pregnant and dropped out to marry and support his family during their senior year. Nate hadn't seen Kidder in almost two years, but that shouldn't matter.

He hoisted himself to his feet again, muscles aching all over his body. Too much had happened just too quickly. His body wasn't equipped for even a fraction of the abuse he had heaped upon it in the last 36 hours. It seems little short of miraculous that he could even stand, much less walk or run.

But run he had, and during his flight away from Lacy and whoever might be working with him, he passed a broken-up old payphone booth, and he realized that his cellphone was back in his apartment. He thought trying to find a working payphone and calling Kidder. He had started back in the direction of the old phone booth to see if it was working when he suddenly brought his feet to a halt.

Stupid! Go the other way. Get as far away from "Them" as possible. There had to be a phone booth somewhere around here that worked. Then he began to doubt his assumption. When was the last time he used a payphone? Exactly! No one did. But there must be some somewhere....

Plodding. Plodding. With more effort than he wanted to exert, he made his legs go up and down, his feet moving along the sidewalk.

Strange thing, adrenalin. It could give you energy from nowhere, but when it wore off, you felt even more exhausted than before.

Up; down.

Up; down.

Up; down.

It was agony, but he kept to it.

His head felt as though it were so heavy it might fall off his shoulders at any moment.

Where the hell was another damn phone booth?

Soon, he'd have to sit and rest again. Soon, but not now. He had to find a phone first. His body pleaded with him to stop; however, he knew that if he gave in to impluse, he might never be able to rise again.

So tired. Need to sleep... Need —

There it was: A booth! Not half a block away on the opposite side of Sixth, and it didn't seem too banged up. Suddenly his adrenalin was working again, and he almost ran across the practically deserted street.

Fishing in his pocket, he came up with a handful of change. Shit, he didn't even know how much a pay call cost anymore. It didn't matter; he had to get this call through. He lifted the receiver and was about to drop the coin in when he realized he hadn't bothered to look up the number yet. Glancing around the filthy booth, he saw no sign of a book. Only shreds of yellow and white pages scattered around the floor. It figured.

He punched up information.

"Directory assistance." The woman sounded fat. Nate didn't know what, but something about her voice made her sound that way.

"Yes, operator. Give me the number please for McBride, last name. First name: Parker. That's Parker McBride. I don't know the address, but there probably isn't more than one."

Why the hell was he being so chatty? Just get on with it. "Checking...minute. Yes, I have a McBride, Parker M. on Whitney."

"That's him!"

"Please deposit one dollar in coins."

"What?"

"The information charge is one dollar."

Nate begrudgingly counted out the coins and dropped them in. He noticed that he only had 55 cents left. If the call also cost a dollar, he wouldn't have enough.

"The number is 846-1173."

"8-4-6-1-1-7-3," he repeated, trying to memorize the number.

"That's correct."

He slammed the receiver down, still repeating the number aloud, softly, while he looked around for the price of a pay call. He found it: 50 cents for 10 minutes. Great!

Quickly, he deposited the coins and waited for the new dial tone. Then, he started dialing.

"Hello!" came the gruff voice from the other end. Nate had almost forgotten he would be waking his old high school buddy from a sound sleep. "Hello!" came the shout again.

But Nate did not respond. He had already dropped the receiver, and was backing out of the phone booth — for, walking directly toward him, not a hundred yards away, was a familiar face.

"Hello, you shithead!" he heard McBride yell just as he vacated the booth, running again.

Panting, about a block down the street, he did permit himself to glance back over his shoulder. He was just in time to see the uniformed cop he'd spoken to at Jonah's reach for the dangling receiver and raise it to his ear.

INTERLUDE E

"Has your little change in procedure paid off yet?"

"Partially, sir. He does seem to be confused, disoriented. I don't believe he understands it yet."

"I see. But...?"

"But he's gotten away from us. Again."

"Did you gain sufficient information to devise a new approach?"

"No, sir, but I have another operation in mind."

CHAPTER ELEVEN

Nate slumped low in the seat, trying to be as inconspicuous as possible. But that wasn't easy on a bus that had only a half dozen or so passengers.

Desperately, he wanted to close his eyes and get a few moments of sleep, but now was not the time. He must be alert — as alert as possible, considering his condition. The cops were on his trail, so he couldn't drop his guard even for a moment.

Staring out the bus window, he watched the smoke drift upward, out of a tall chimney at the Prequet Brewery. The old brick structure was dingy with age, showing signs that it had been too long without proper care. But it was typical of this part of town.

Kidder McBride, he thought, trying to focus an image of his old school friend, but the picture inside his head was fuzzy and distorted. Finally, he gave up trying.

Anyway, at least, he knew Kidder was home.

"Mama, this is Kidder."

"Well, bring him on in, Sonny." She studied McBride carefully.

"Heard lots 'bout you. Sonny's always sayin' somethin' 'bout Kidder this 'n Kidder that. Guess you two perty good friends?"

Kidder smiled. "Yes, ma'am, we shore are!"

She smiled. "That's fine, boy. I'm glad you come over to spend the night with Sonny tonight."

Nate felt himself growing impatient. "Come on, Kidder. Got something to show you."

He grabbed his friend by the arm and began to drag him away from Mama.

"What'd you do that for?" Kidder asked when Nate had closed the door to the room he had once shared with Otis.

"Had to. If I didn't, Mama would talk your ear off. Anyway, I got something you gonna wanta see."

Kidder grinned. "Yeah? What is it?"

Nate pulled the battered, old cardboard box out from under his bed. "Here!" he said, beaming broadly.

"Comic books!" Parker shouted, kneeling on one knee, staring at the box's contents. "Must be a hundred!"

"Nearly 'bout two hunderd."

Kidder began to dig into the box with both hands.

"Whoa!" Nate shouted. "Them's all sorted out. My brother always kept 'em straight."

"These was his?" Kidder asked.

"Some of 'em — well, most of 'em, maybe. We was partners."

"Oh."

"But I don't have no partner no more," Nate added.

Kidder looked up, a hopeful glint in his eyes.

"Would you like to be my partner now?"

His friend's smile could not have been any wider. "Would I? You betcha, I would."

Carefully now, Kidder began to remove the comics from the box and stack them around the floor in piles, separated by titles. When he'd finished, he looked up at Nate who was still sitting on the edge of his bed. "Know something, Nate? You're the best friend a dude could ever have."

The fact that Kidder was a year older never got in the way of their friendship. By the time they were in high school, Nate had caught up with Kidder, and they were together until that senior year when Kidder dropped out to get married.

Nate watched the rows of factory windows float by. It would have been easier if Kidder didn't live all the way across town. Oh, well, maybe this would make it more difficult for Lacy to track him down. Maybe it would give him at least enough time to find out what all this was about.

The bus pulled to a stop, and Nate watched an elderly white woman, laden with a heavy paper sack full of what appeared to be cooking utensils get off at the rear door.

Suddenly, the fear gripped him. He felt drawn to the front of the vehicle, and he fought with his impulses just to remain in his seat. A young, dark-complexed woman, probably Hispanic, was entering the bus, but she seemed to be moving in slow motion, as Lacy had fallen and as the awning had come down, crushing Casta. Nate watched as she planted a second foot inside the vehicle, while, at the same time, her right hand began to move across in front of her body toward her purse. He looked up at her face and saw that she had a non-commital stare in her eyes, as if she were walking around in a daze. Maybe she was on something "heavy." Her hand had not quiet reached her purse yet, but he was having trouble keeping his eyes on the scene now, for he felt the first twinges of one of his headaches. His right hand shot up to his forehead, and he tried to rub the pain away, without success. Slowly he lowered his fingers to his eyelids and rubbed them vigorously. When he removed his hand, he saw that the woman now seemed somewhat out of focus, but he could tell that she had only begun to snap the purse open.

Boom.

Boom.

Boom.

Cannons. Inside his head. Exploding shells inside his skull.

He closed his eyes and shook his head vigorously. When he opened them again, he discovered he could no longer make out details of the scene transpiring at the front of the bus.

Crash.

Crash.

All around him they were falling.

Crash.

A whole forest of trees crashing down inside his head.

"No!" he heard himself scream.

But that would not forestall it. He knew what was coming, and he wouldn't have — *couldn't* have it — now. Not with those vultures on his tail. He had to know what it all meant. He had to!

His eyes were open. He knew they were, but he couldn't see anything. Just a gray mist. He was surrounded by grayness. All of life had become a panorama of gray. No details. No movement. No nothing. Just gray.

"Stop it!" he shouted. Or, at least, he thought he was shouting. But he wasn't sure.

Now he felt himself drifting, floating along in the gray world. He had a feeling there were people around him — all around him — but he didn't know that for certain. He could feel breathing on his skin, or it seemed that way. Someone was talking — no, everyone was talking — though their voices were strange and the sounds undecipherable.

Where am I? he wanted to scream, but he held back because, for some reason, he felt as though he had no mouth.

What's going on?

No one answered.

Help me, please!
And a face began to take shape out of the mist.
Mama! Make it stop. Make the bad dream stop.
But the face wasn't Mama's.
Nate tried to focus on the face, to block out the grayness that surrounded it.
"Hang on, Nate!"
Who...
said...
that?
"I did," the face said. "You've got to hang on."
What...?
"Hang on..."
Who...?
The face began to come closer. Now, he could tell it was a woman. It was —
Casta!
"Hang on!"
Then she was gone — absorbed back into the grayness.
No! Not again. Stolen from him again. *Come back. Casta!*
The face was gone, but he could still hear the voice. "You're on your own, now, Nate."
No-o-o-o-o!
"What did you say?"
The grayness — it was gone!
"Did you say something to me?"
Nate shook his head, trying to clear it.
"Oh, I beg your pardon. I thought you said something."
He was standing on the sidewalk in the front of a bakery. A white, square-faced man in a navy-blue business suit was facing him, and he saw that there were people all around them. The man shrugged and turned away. Nate squinted. The sun was hurting his

eyes.

The sun? But it shouldn't be... He shouldn't be...

However, it was, and he was. The sun was almost directly overhead, and he was standing on a crowded sidewalk, not riding a nearly empty bus during the wee hours of the morning.

He began to move along with the crowd, trying to remember. He could bring back memory of the grayness and of Casta and of the Hispanic woman moving in slow motion, but there was nothing to account for this.

Maybe he was, maybe he *really* was going off the deep end. That would account for all that had been happening to him.

No! Not all. It wouldn't account for the fact that someone was trying to kill him for some unknown reason.

And even if he was going crazy — if he *already* was crazy — he couldn't turn himself in for treatment now. Not until he got the pieces to fit together.

He felt a hunger pang and looked around for a place to eat. A McDonald's was right down the street, so he stumbled toward it.

"Could I help someone?" the young, freckled-faced waitress asked.

Nate stepped up to the counter. "Gimme two cheeseburgers, some fries and a Pepsi."

"Is Coke okay?" she asked.

He nodded.

She stepped away from the counter and started gathering up the items he'd ordered.

Another blackout. He must've blacked out again on the bus. Yes, that would explain it. And while he was out, he'd had some wild dreams. Nightmares. Everybody had nightmares. You didn't have to be nuts to have nightmares. In fact, he'd read somewhere that nightmares were a safety valve, letting off anxiety so that people didn't flip out. Sure, that was it.

No, it wasn't. He'd better stop kidding himself. Blacking out was one thing and having nightmares, too. But that didn't explain the slow-motion "visions" he'd been having or how he got out of that bus.

"Are you alright, sir?"

"What?"

"Here's your order."

"Thank you," he mumbled, reaching across the counter and pulling the sack and cup toward him. His left hand was reaching into his back pocket.

"That comes to — "

Oh, my God! His wallet was gone!

He felt his jaw sag and his eyes go wide.

"Are you sure you're alright?"

Alright? No! Hell, no, he wasn't alright! Nothing was right. People were trying to kill him; his girlfriend has already been murdered; he was blacking out and seeing things and thinking things that didn't make sense; and, now, to top it off, his money was missing.

Without replying, he whirled and ran from the restaurant.

What else could happen to him? He remembered asking himself that a few years ago, also.

"It ain't th' end of th' world, Sonny. You'll get over it." But how? First his best friend quit school and got married. Now this.

He looked up at Mama. "That's easy for you to say."

Almost immediately he knew that was the wrong thing. He shouldn't have said it. He could already see the hurt in Mama's eyes. Slowly, he pushed himself to a sitting position on the edge of his bed.

"There'll be other girls. Mark my word, boy. 'Fore long, you'll have 'em runnin' after you."

"Sure, Mama."

"It'll happen. You'll see."

"But, Mama, I don't want it to happen. I don't care for it to happen. All I want is Eli back."

"'Fraid you can't have that."

She was so right. Why did Mama have to be right all the time?

"Thing was, I didn't even know she's goin' with anybody else."

Mama nodded.

"And here, she ups and runs off and marries Dave Blume. Why didn't she at least have the decency to tell me about him...?"

Mama shook her head, making little clicking sounds with her mouth.

"...And here I go over to her house for our date, and she ain't there. 'Well, where is she?' I asks her mama, whose been cryin' — I can tell — but I can't get nothing outa her. Finally, her daddy comes to th' door and tells me I better go on back home 'cause Eli run off with Dave."

Mama put an arm around his back, and he looked over at her. Why couldn't all women be like Mama?

"Like I said minute ago: Ain't th' end a th' world, you know. You'll get over it in time."

And there had been several other girls after Eli before he'd settled on Casta last year.

Back on the street, he felt his stomach reminding him that he had left his food behind. No money — no eats. But how could he make his stomach understand?

Even more importantly, how would he get over — and out of — the mess he was now in?

The faces around him were a jumble. People racing past him at breakneck speed. Coming. Going. And not a one familiar. In fact, as he looked around him, he realized that he didn't even recognize where he was. He'd never been in this part of town before.

Lost, too! On top of everything else, he was lost.

Suddenly, he remembered where he'd been going when he'd blacked out, and he knew he needed help more than ever now — now that he didn't even have any money. But first, he needed to find out where he was.

Looking around, he spotted an open-air newspaper stand just up the street, so he headed for it. He stepped up to the vendor to inquire as to his whereabouts. He was opening his mouth to speak when his eyes fell on the front page of a paper immediately in front of him.

Gasping, he staggered back. For he'd just read the dateline. Somehow, he'd lost two days out of his life!

CHAPTER TWELVE

At least, Nate knew where he was now, even if he didn't know how he got here.

Or what had happened to the last two days.

He was all of five miles from Kidder's house, but he wondered if he weren't even further away from reality.

There seemed little left to do but head out on foot. Without money, he couldn't even ride the bus. His hunger pangs had quietened down now, having been replaced by an occasional growl from his stomach. He wondered when he'd last eaten. Had he tasted anything at all during the past two days?

The throng was thinning out now, since apparently the lunch hour was over and all the office workers had returned to their desks and computers. And, actually, walking wasn't bad today. The weather was pleasant: a little cooler than two days ago and the humidity was lower. All-in-all, he might even have enjoyed the stroll if he could have turned off his mind.

Nate tried to concentrate on his surroundings.

At the corner, he saw a glass installation truck pull to a halt. Two men climbed out and started to work at removing a rather large piece. A showcase window, no doubt. Maybe vandals had broken something. But Nate couldn't wait around to see.

They were on his trail. Nate knew they were following him. They had to be.

A young white woman was leading her small son across the street when he yanked his hand free and ran directly in front of an on-coming concrete truck. Somehow, the driver stopped just in time. The woman jerked the child up, spitting profanities at both the boy and the truck driver.

Maybe he should have killed Lacy. That would have made one less adversary to face.

An ice cream van rumbled past, playing its merry jingle. A sure sign of warm weather. But it must be going in to make a pick-up. Surely the driver wouldn't be peddling his cones in a commercial district.

Where were they? Why hadn't they finished him off already?

A yellow cab stopped suddenly to take on a passenger, and a checkered one which had been following in the lane beside the yellow one whipped sharply right and took the tail light off the first vehicle. Both the drivers jumped out, shaking fists and swearing at each other. The man who had been about to get into the yellow cab chose a third one, one marked "City Cab" and rode away while the drivers of the first two vehicles continued their argument.

Maybe he should really get off the street. He was terribly conspicuous out here. What if Lacy or Corley came along? Hell, any cop might haul him in, for that matter.

A crowd seemed to be gathering in front of the courthouse, and there was a lot of shouting, none of which was understandable. There were no placards and the group was clearly interracial, so he couldn't guess what cause they were espousing.

But it wasn't the "hauling in" that he dreaded. He just had a feeling that if they found him, there would be no visit to the jail, no booking, and no chance for him to "plead."

The slumlord housing had set in, as he was passing out of the commercial district into a border area filled with dingy shops, abandoned and burned-out buildings, and ragged children, both black and white. Nate could remember the rioting that had occurred when he was very young, and he knew this area had been hard hit. Some of the buildings had now set in their present state of decay for more than a decade.

God, was it even worth it? Maybe he should simply give himself up.

A little black girl of about four was dragging a mangy-looking puppy down the street. The girl had one end of a stick in her hands and the dog had the other end in its mouth. She was shouting at the animal and backing up down the sidewalk, and the creature was skidding along, growling and shaking its head from side to side. Nate had to jump out of their way to avoid colliding with the small pair.

Give himself up? For what? What had he done? Sure, he'd slugged Lacy, but the bastard was about to pull a gun on him and shoot him down, no doubt.

He was now in an area of individual homes. Small, old, and ugly, but they were single-family homes, similar to the one he'd grown up in and had lived in with Mama until three years ago.

They were probably patroling the entire city by now, looking for him. Maybe he'd even made the "most wanted" list.

An abundant woman of dark complexion dressed in the traditional "washer woman" outfit of cotton-print dress with a rag tied around her head was energetically sweeping her walk and singing, "When th' Roll is Called Up Yonder." Nate smiled as he passed her, but she apparently didn't even take note of his presence.

If he could only —

Damn! Speak of the Devil!

Nate's eyes darted about wildly, then he made a dash for a hedge row at the front of a "gun barrel" house with dusty, peeling gray paint. He lunged behind the hedge, keeping his head low, breathing rapidly.

After several seconds in that uncomfortable crouch position, he allowed himself to raise his head slightly, just enough to peek over the top of the hedge and determine that the cop car was proceeding on down the street past him. He saw that it was almost out of sight already, but he also observed that the woman who'd been sweeping and singing was looking directly toward him.

A few seconds later, he stood up, dusted himself off and walked back out to the sidewalk. The woman was still staring.

Hell, what did he care? Damn bitch. She'd been "too good" to acknowledge his existence a moment ago, and now she was gorging her eyes. Well, he'd just play along.

"Hello!" he shouted, waving at her.

She wrinkled up her brow, shook her head, and went back to her sweeping.

Let her think what she wanted to, he told himself, almost laughing. Then he remembered his situation, and he knew he certainly had no cause for laughter.

It shouldn't be much further to Kidder's house. The territory was getting very familiar. He had passed into what the two of them used to call their "stomping ground."

Passing Ferguson's Grocery, he almost bumped into a fiftyish-looking, white, bread-truck driver as the other exited the store. The man gave Nate a sharp look.

"Sorry," Nate offered, though he was certain it wasn't his fault.

"'Zokay," the other replied, hurrying on toward his truck.

A few seconds later, Nate heard the man call out again. "Hey, bud!"

Nate whirled and stared at the bread man.

"This yores?" The man was holding a small black comb. Nate felt in his right rear pocket. It was empty.

"Yeah. Thanks," he shouted back, returning toward the other at a brisk pace.

He reached for the comb, but the other man tugged back on it, refusing to let go. "You kids really oughta be more careful," he mumbled.

Suddenly, Nate felt himself consumed with hatred and disgust toward the sniveling idiot standing before him. He squinted his eyes, and the man collapsed to his knees. Simultaneously, his skin seemed to become transparent. Nate could still see the other man's face, now twisted in agony, but he could also see a strange jumble of scenes and people and faces superimposed in front of the driver. Nate closed his eyes and the man's face disappeared, but the jumble did not.

Slowly, in what proved to be a very painful experience, Nate forced a refocusing of his attention. The throbbing inside his forehead was returning, but gradually the strange images began to fade away, to be replaced by that of his mother the last time he'd seen her, lying in her hospital bed — turning his life over to Casta!

"O-o-o-oh, damn! Holy Shit!" The agonizing scream from the bread man broke his concentration, and Nate opened his eyes to see the other holding his head and leaping into his vehicle. Seconds later, the driver and truck sped away.

INTERLUDE F

"He's been out of sight for two days?"

"Yes, sir. But I'm positive he'll surface again, soon. We've even pinpointed the probable location he'll appear in. When he does, we'll nab him. We have everything in position."

"Just see that it works this time, Panther. Time is running out."

CHAPTER THIRTEEN

A familiar face appeared on the other side of the screen door.

"Hey, Tibman! Come on in."

Nate stumbled through the door which the other swung open. He'd been "Tibman" to McBride almost as long as McBride had been "Kidder" to him.

Kidder held out both hands, palms up, a broad grin on his face. "Man, you're a sight for — well, let me look at you. You're just a sight. What th' fuck happened to *you*, bro?"

The other's hands dropped back to his side and Nate slumped into a battered, old easy chair. Kidder sat across from him in a creaky rocker. The grin had disappeared.

"You wouldn't believe me if I told you, Kidder."

"Try me, man. I'm all ears."

Nate let his eyes wander around the small room as he tried to pull his thoughts together. A small, hand-made "plaque" of sorts hanging on the wall opposite him attracted his attention, but he didn't need to strain to read its rough printing. He had a chunk of wood, back in his apartment somewhere which had the same words — words written by two young boys half a lifetime ago. The words formed a pact of friendship and loyalty. As he sat staring at the rough wood, which seemed somehow different from all the other wall-hangings, more in focus almost, he allowed himself to smile.

"Well, ain't you gonna tell me *somethin'?*"

He glanced around at Kidder. "What? Oh, yeah. I was just lookin' at what you got hangin' over there." Nate nodded toward the plaque.

But Kidder seemed to know what he was referring to without looking toward it. "Yeah, been a long time, ain't it, Tibman?"

"Sure has."

There was another moment of silence, but this time Nate sat with his eyes closed.

"You been takin' heat from th' Man?" Kidder asked, finally.

Nate opened his eyes. "Maybe. I'm not sure?"

"What you talkin' 'bout? You *ain't sure?*"

"I'm not, Kidder. I don't know what's going on."

"Well, is the law after you or not?"

"I guess you could say it is."

"Listen, man, you tryin' to give me the run-around? Why you doin' this to me? You come in here lookin' like you're half beat to death, and you won't even say nothin' 'bout it."

Nate shrugged and, for the first time since coming to himself on the street, he took account of his appearance. His dress shirt was filthy and wrinkled all over; one of the buttons was missing; and the pocket was ripped. The suit pants were, likewise, in bad condition, with the powder blue turned brown with dirt in several spots and a snag in the fabric over his left knee.

"Sorry," he said at last. "I'm just wiped out. I may not have slept in two or three days."

"What *are* you talkin' 'bout, bro? You *ain't sure* and now you say you *may not* have slept in a coupla days. That don't make no kinda sense."

"You're right, Kidder. I'm...just...tired."

"Then maybe I better find you a bed quick, and we can talk tomor. I sure ain't gettin' nothin' outa you, now."

Kidder began to rise, but Nate waved him back down.

"No, I gotta tell you, Kidder. Maybe together we can figure this thing out."

"That's what I'm hopin'."

"Good. That's my man. I knew I could count on you."

Nate paused, caught his breath, then plunged in. "Kidder, somebody's tryin' to kill me, but I don't know who and I don't know why."

"For real?"

"Yeah, but that ain't all that's hap'nin'. All kinds a weird things been hap'nin' to me."

"Like what?"

"Like I been havin' headaches and blackouts. The last time I was out for two days."

"*Two days*? That's a hell of a long time. What happened?"

"I don't know. I just come to wandering around the streets."

Kidder's mouth sagged open.

"But that's not the worst. The worst is: They got Casta. They killed her — tryin' to get me. I know that's what it was."

Now, Kidder leaned forward in his seat, staring into Nate's eyes. "Who? They got who?"

"*Casta!*" There was a look of incredulity on Nate's face, which slowly melted away. "Oh, I forgot. You don't know her. Casta's my woman. Casta Jordan. We live together or, rather, we did."

He dropped his head into his hands and stared down at the rough wood floor. A few seconds later he looked up, tears trickling down his cheeks.

"Shit, Kidder. She was some woman. *Some* woman! And them bastards destroyed her."

Nate could see sorrow in Kidder's eyes, too, but his friend offered no comment.

"Christ dammit, I know I'm not makin' much sense, but let me try." He gritted his teeth and closed his eyes, trying again to organize his thoughts. "We were out at a theater. We were just comin' out when the roof caved in on her. She never had a chance."

Kidder patted him lightly on the knee.

"No, it's not what you think, Kidder. *They* did it. By God, they did it to her, and I'm gonna find 'em and make 'em pay for it."

"Anything you say, bro."

Nate jerked away from the other's hand and jumped up.

"Dammit, Kidder, don't patronize me! I tell you it happened that way." His eyes were mere slits, and his teeth were clenched. He began to slowly pace among the ragged living room furniture. Finally, he turned back to his silent friend, who started to speak, but Nate held up a hand and resumed his previous seat.

"No, I say *it happened.* I saw it with my own eyes. I saw...I saw — something!"

"What? You saw what?"

"Somehow, Kidder, I saw how they did it. There were two of them. I know it. One of them was positioned on the roof of the building across the street from the theater waiting for us. When we came out, he...he must've — yeah, that's right, that's what he did! — *signaled* the guy on the roof of the theater above us. And it was the second one who dropped it on Casta. It was intended for me, but I saw it all and jumped back."

"You mean you saw the guy across the street signalin' the other'n?"

"*Sure!* I saw that *and* the other guy, too!"

"How? If one of 'em was on the roof above you, how could you see him?"

"I tell you Kidder, I *saw him*! Dammit, I know what I saw!"

"Okay, okay." Kidder raised both hands and slid back in his seat.

Nate rested an elbow on his thigh and his forehead on his fingertips. "Yeah, *how* did I see him?"

"That's what I just asked."

"I don't know, Kidder. God, I don't know. Just let me think." A pause, then: "But I *know* what I saw. I'm not crazy; I can't be. It really happened, I tell you."

"I've heard enough, Tibman. You're worn out. You've got to rest. Anybody can see that." Kidder began to rise again. "Let's get you to bed. We can talk in th' mo'nin'."

"Shit, man, I'm tryin' to think. Would you *just leave me alone* so I can sort this thing out?"

"Sure, Tibman, if that's what you want." Kidder began to step away from his guest, toward the rear of the house.

"Wait, Kidder. Don't pay me no mind right now. I'm just tired — "

"That's why — "

"*Shut up*...please, Kidder. Please just come back over here and sit down and help me figure this thing out. We used to be a team. Wudn't nothin' could stop Kidder 'n' Tibman. Ever'body knew that. You remember, don't you?" Nate looked into Kidder's eyes, but he found no joy there, only a far-away, sad look.

However, Kidder did seat himself once more.

"How'd I do it, Kidder?"

"Search me?"

He tried to focus his memory on that night — two nights ago. Two nights which had somehow been taken from him and he had no accounting for.

"I...saw — it was wire! The roof or the awning or whatever you wanna call it was held up by wires. They musta already knocked out the real supports. Then, they cut the wire, and the whole thing dropped — on Casta."

"How do you know that, Tibman?"

"I just know, that's all. I *saw* it! Remember, I told you I saw it."

"But how?"

"With my own two I eyes, I — no, no, I didn't! I couldn't a done that, could I?"

But Kidder said nothing more.

"No, I guess not," Nate added, finally. "Tired, so damn tired..."

"Sometimes your mind plays tricks on you, Tibman. It does on all a us. Why don't you just get some rest? Ever'thin'll look better in till mo'nin'."

"Maybe you're right, Kidder. I'm wiped out. I didn't know how exhausted I was till got here."

Now, Nate began to rise. "I just wonder when was the last time I slept. I know I wudn't out for two days. Something musta happened, but I just can't remember."

Kidder slapped him lightly on the back. "Come on, bro. We got a bed all ready for you."

Slowly, Nate made his way over to the hand-made plaque hanging on the dingy, wallpapered walls and studied it. Somehow, it seemed cleaner than everything else hanging around it, as if it had just been dusted, maybe. His eyes focused on the words inscribed by two young friends: "We Nathan Tibbetts and Parker McBride make this pack of brotherhud and frendship for ever. Til death do we keep it." And it was signed with two initials only: "T." and "K."

Looking around at his friend, Nate tried to smile. "Weren't much at spelling, were we?"

But Kidder was staring at the front door. "Huh?" he asked, looking back around at Nate. "Oh, yeah, guess not, bro. Come on, you better get yourself in bed. We can talk 'bout that kinda stuff tomor."

Nate nodded. "Right.... And I really gotta have your help, Kidder. I gotta figure this thing out before it drives me nuts."

"Sure...tomor. Come on." He led Nate into a bedroom, which was, though not decorated with the best of furnishing, at least clean, and even the bed was made. As Nate slipped his shoes off and pulled back the covers, he noticed that the sheets seemed clean and crisp. He dropped his head on the soft pillow, and he felt his heavy eyelids closing. But something new was bothering him, something just below his level of consciousness.

He saw Kidder quietly slipping out of the room, and he knew how badly he needed to sleep. But he still wanted to talk.

"Where's Clarice and little Tyrone?" he asked.

"Oh, them? Well, they gone over to Clarice's mama's. They'll be back after while. You just get some rest."

"But Kidder, where you two gonna sleep? This is your bed, right?"

"Uh, yeah, but that don't matter, Tibman. We'll sleep on the couch."

Nate shoved the sheet off his weary body and forced himself into a sitting position. "Not right. I can't take your bed. What'll Clarice think when she comes home and finds me sleepin' here? I can sleep on the couch."

He swung his legs off the bed and tried to stand, but Kidder's palm was pressing against his chest.

"No, Tibman, you sleep here. Clarice won't need the bed. We won't need it. She ain't comin' back tonight. She's gonna stay over there till tomor. You just go to sleep. I'll be okay, brother."

Nate let his body drop back onto the bed. "You sure? She really won't be back tonight? You really positive?"

"I told you that, didn't I? You ever know me to lie to you? Now come on — sleep."

"Well..."

"If you wanna know, you damn nosy bastard, we had a little argument a while ago. She'll be gone all night. That's what she does when it happens." Kidder paused, and Nate noticed that his skin seemed to be getting transparent as the bread man's had.

No, he couldn't let this happen again. He had to get control of himself before he started seeing weird things. He couldn't let it happen, not in front of Kidder.

"Okay, Kidder, I believe you. Go on. I'll sleep, I promise." His old school buddy began to tiptoe toward the door, and Nate noticed his features becoming more substantial-looking. Good, it was working.

"Just one more thing," he added, as Kidder was about to close the door. "Wake me up early, okay? I gotta talk to you before you leave tomorrow. Will you wake me, *please* — ?"

"I'll do it, Tibman. Now, *sleep!*"

The images had begun to appear again as Kidder pulled the door closed, but Nate concentrated on fighting them off, and finally, he felt sleep begin to drift in. But he wasn't completely under. Something inside his weary brain refused to let go completely. Nate found that he had to fight with himself just to let sleep come.

Oh, sweet sleep, beautiful sleep. He *had* to sleep.

Slowly, his mind began to clear, and he felt himself start to drift again. He felt himself begin to fall. Then he was plummeting.

Down.

Down.

Down.

There was no bottom. Nothing to stop him.

No! Stop it!

"Stop it!" He felt this body convulse and suddenly he was sitting up in the bed. Shaking his groggy head, he tried to throw off the nightmare image. He took his right hand and massaged his temple, then slowly settled himself back onto the pillow.

"Got to sleep," he heard himself whisper, and he realized how foolish he would sound to another who might enter and hear him — hear him trying to convince his own body to relax.

But it was working. Gradually, he felt sleep begin to slip in once more, and this time he felt more at peace. He was almost completely under when he heard it. At first, he didn't recognize the sound, but he knew he'd heard it before somewhere. What was it? It was... It was...

The sound of a telephone being dialed. But he was too weary to focus on the conversation. All he could make out was, "he's ready," before sleep finally overtook him.

INTERLUDE G

"My men have just received word. They should have him within a half hour."

"What makes you think this operation stands more of a chance than the others?"

"I've designed it especially to take advantage of his disorientation."

CHAPTER FOURTEEN

The theater's awning was crashing down onto her. Again? How? How could this be occurring? He distinctly remembered it happening before.

But it *was* happening again. He could hear it. The same loud crashing, and...

The sound of voices.

Wait! The voices were new. He hadn't heard them the first time.

And the noise didn't sound quite right either. It sounded more like a door crashing open and feet running.

Then he could feel fingertips wrap around his forearm, and he struggled to open his eyelids. Finally, as he felt himself being jerked upright in the bed, they swung open.

A man was standing beside the bed on which Nate now knelt — a man dressed in a perfect-fitting, gray business suit but wearing a dark ski mask over his face. The man was fishing in his coat pocket for something. A second later, the man removed a handkerchief and shoved it into Nate's open mouth. Nate tried to reach around with his right hand and remove the gag, but he felt his arm being restrained. He felt it being jerked behind his back, along with the left. Swinging his head around to stare over his right shoulder, he could see a second man similarly dressed, except that his ski mask appeared, in the dim light of the bedroom, to be red. Nate could feel his hands being forced together and something encircling his wrists. There was a distinct "click," then a second one, and the man in the red mask nodded to the man in front, who placed a hand under his left arm and began to hoist him upward. A second later, he felt a hand slip under his right armpit, as well. His feet hit the floor, and the men led him through the open bedroom door.

"I'm sorry, Tibman," he heard someone say, but the words felt like they were inside his own head. As he was being led through the maze of furniture, he scanned the room quickly, finally finding Kidder in one corner by the television set. He couldn't see the other's lips moving, but Nate could still hear the words. "I didn't want to. Honest, Tibman. I didn't want to — "

Suddenly, he felt himself jerked to a halt, and the first man, the man in the darker mask, reached into another coat pocket and removed a dark strip of cloth. This one he tied tightly around Nate's eyes. Then he felt the man's fingers under his armpit again, and he was being led once more.

" — but they made me. Don't you see: They was gonna kill Clarice and Tyrone. I had to protect them. What else — "

He heard a car door opening, and felt himself being thrust inside. Once in the vehicle, he tried to sit up, but he felt himself being forced down. Down into what must be the vehicle's floorboard.

" — could I do? I didn't want to. I wish I could talk to you, and tell you that. You'd understand — "

Lying on his side, he felt cramped, his back against the rear of the front seat, his stomach against the back seat. He felt something shoving against his shoulder, and he caught a whiff which told him it was a man's foot, a stinking foot, strong enough to smell repellent even surrounded by a shoe.

" — I know you would. You always understood me better'n anybody else. I hoped you wouldn't show up, so I wouldn't haveta do this. But then — "

A car door slammed. He both heard it and felt the vibrations. A second later, he heard another door open, then the vehicle's engine roar into action. A jerking motion told him that the car was pulling away.

" — you came. I tried to think of something, but I couldn't. I been worried sick about Clarice. Tibman, I wanted — "

The vibrations and swaying told him that the car was moving swiftly, and swinging around corners, both left and right. He felt a churning in his insides, but he wasn't sure if it was caused by the movement of the car, the fact that he hadn't eaten possibly in more than two days, or from what was happening to him now. His mind still felt groggy, as if it were clogged with all kinds of conflicting thoughts and emotions.

" — to tell you, but I couldn't. Oh, shit, what have I done? What have I — ?"

Enough! He'd heard enough of that drivel.

Shut up. You cowardly asshole!

Suddenly, his mind began to clear, but he almost wished it hadn't.

God! What was happening to him now? Where were these goons taking him? And how had they — ?

Oh, shit! He remembered now. That damn telephone he'd left dangling — that had to be it! When he'd spied that cop, he'd just dropped it and ran. Going to Kidder's house was the worse place he could have gone.

Nate felt a trickle of sweat on his forehead and his cheeks. There was a dryness in his mouth, too, and he couldn't swallow whatever that was in his throat.

Damn! Now he'd done it. He'd signed himself out for good. But why? Why was this happening?

And where were they taking him? Nate began to concentrate on the rumble of the car as it jerked and swerved, throwing him first against the back seat, then against the front. The hump in the vehicle's middle was quite uncomfortable, but he bowed his mid-section and tried to ignore it.

Gradually, he began to "see." He had the impression that he was sitting in the front seat behind the wheel of a car as he jerked along, charging down an unfamiliar street.

No, that wasn't right! He wasn't in the driver's seat. He was sitting in the back seat watching everything, and he was feeling a peculiar annoyance with the way the driver was operating the car. Nevertheless, he was determined to follow instructions and not speak. He was a professional, and he could keep silent even if his life depended on him talking, and it might just at that, with the way Lynx was driving.

Wait, that wasn't right either. He was having trouble seeing now. He could still see the street ahead, but it was blurred and out of focus, like...like —

Like he was seeing double!

But the whole experience was hurting his head. Nate squeezed his eyelids closed tightly, but nothing happened. He still saw the image as clearly as before. Or, rather, as blurred as before.

Gradually, he felt his mind begin to wander. No, not wander, exactly. More like it was being pulled along in a direction he hadn't planned to take. In fact, he had no control...

How had he let himself get roped into another assignment with Otter? The man was a jerk. No foresight. He never thought anything through. And he'd been put in charge. Now, that was really stupid. Somebody upstairs had really flipped out this time, putting an important job like this under Otter's control.

And he'd better watch out, too. Otter's reputation didn't make him the safest partner to work with either. At least a third of his partners had wound up six feet under. Oh, what the hell, that wasn't likely to happen this time. Not in this kind of operation.

Nate shook his head vigorously, trying to clear it. Then he felt the foot on his shoulder pressing down hard against his flesh. Christ, was this goon trying to crush him with his foot? The pressure was making his muscles throb, and he wanted to yell something at the bastard. But the damn gag in his mouth wouldn't let much sound escape, he realized, and he wasn't inclined to waste his energy on something as futile as grunting. Besides, maybe that was what this guy wanted. He wasn't going to give him the satisfaction of hearing anything. Gradually, Nate could feel the pressure increasing, but he concentrated on refocusing his mind, trying to withstand the pain without making a sound — directing his thoughts toward the anger and hatred he felt for the bastard who held him pinned down.

Then his vision of the road ahead vanished suddenly.

"Oh, fuck!" he heard someone shout from the back seat at the same instant he felt the foot jerk away completely off his shoulder.

Nate tried to relax as much as possible. These goons had kidnapped him for a reason; he didn't know what, any more than he could explain the other strange things that had been happening to him. However, they hadn't just rushed into Kidder's house and gunned him down. Why? Obviously they were taking him somewhere for a purpose. He didn't know what that purpose was, but surely it wasn't simply to slay him; otherwise, why would they be bothering with all this?

And another thing: How were these guys connected with the bunch who'd been trying to kill him? Were they the same? That didn't make any sense, though nothing had recently.

He wanted to work up the intensity of anger and hatred he'd felt after Casta's murder, but he couldn't. Maybe he was just too tired. For some reason, he couldn't even sustain his fear of these two.

His mind began to wander again, and...

Damn piss, and to think he was stuck on an assignment with a jerk who couldn't even follow the basic rule of silence. He didn't know why Panther had imposed the rule this time, but if Panther wanted it, then Panther got it. How did that dumb poem go: "Ours not to reason why. Ours but to do or die"? Or was it "...do and die"? What did it matter, anyway? Nobody was going to die this time....

What the hell was wrong with his leg? Shit — never had a muscle spasm like that before. Not with a pain that felt like a tongue of fire licking him. And with that snitch Lynx sitting up front, he was liable to be reported. Someday, he'd have to take care of Lynx like he'd done with Hyena and Margay and Bear and the others. Couldn't have sneaky little bastards like them running around loose....

Nate felt the car pulling to a halt, and he saw a blurry vision of well-kept lawn and a rather abundant, white, two-story house, set back off the street a ways. No other house was immediately visible.

A hand was wrapped around one of his arms, and he felt himself being pulled up. He obliged, helping raise himself to a sitting position on the car's seat, then he slid in the direction of the hand on his arm. It wouldn't help any to struggle right now, not when he was handcuffed and gagged and blindfolded. Besides, perhaps what he needed most was information. He had to find out what all this was about. Maybe if he cooperated, he might learn something. Otherwise, he would be in no position to fight back. How could he if he didn't know who to fight or even why he was fighting? Maybe inside this house he'd find enough answers to defend himself.

As he reached the car door, he felt the second man's hand wrap around his other arm, and he found himself being escorted along as he had been in exiting from Kidder's house.

What was the big deal about this guy? What was Panther up to now? He'd never been sent out on an assignment as weird as this one? This guy must know something really important if Control was taking these kinds of pains with him. Still, rumor had it that...

This was the same nigger he and Bear had taken on in that alley. He was sure of it. Why was Panther changing the game plan? Their orders then had been to extinguish him. Why were they keeping him alive, now? So what if Panther wanted to talk to him? Why now? And another thing about this one troubled him: He'd been a hellcat that night. Now, he was a pussycat. Something funny was going on, and he was beginning not to like it...

Nate shook his head again, half dragging his feet as he moved up the concrete walk. The two men at his side picked up his slack, partially supporting him. He tried to concentrate on reality, to purge his mind of the confusing conglomeration of strange thoughts. Finally, he decided to focus simply on walking and to see what he could pick up through the use of the other senses still available to him.

The hand on his right arm, then the one on his left tugged back on him, drawing him to a halt. But not for long. He heard a door open, and once again, the hands were pulling him forward. His feet touched carpet, and Nate felt himself swing sharply to the right. Down a hallway maybe. Another pause. Another door opening.

Suddenly, he felt himself being shoved, and he fell

onto a thickly padded carpet. The door closed, and there was a click. Nate knew that he had been placed in a cell of sorts — a carpeted cell, but a cell, nonetheless. His hands were still handcuffed behind his back, and the gag and blindfold were still in place. Why did they need to lock the door, too?

For a few seconds, he lay where he had fallen, face down on the carpeting. Then, slowly, he rolled over onto his side and sat up. It took some effort to climb to his feet with his hands fastened behind his back and without his eyes to guide him from stumbling into something as he rose, but eventually he made it. Almost immediately, he knocked over what he was sure was a metal chair. More cautiously now, he began to edge his way around the room, discovering a table as well as a plush sofa. Gradually, he lowered himself onto the sofa, but he felt very uncomfortable, with his hands restrained behind him. Finally, he stretched out on his side, the most comfortable position he could find. He thought of trying to sleep, remembering how tired he had been he'd lain down at Kidder's.

Kidder! That was the meaning of the phone call he had heard. His old "buddy" had turned him in. But to whom? And why? What was going on? Why did everybody know more than he did?

He began to slowly open and close his fists, and each time he closed them, he squeezed the fingertips more tightly against the tender flesh of his palms. He felt his fingernails biting into the skin and also the sting of punctured flesh, but he kept it up. He wanted to scream, to vent his anger in a profane vocalization, but the gag prevented him. He felt his body begin to tremble all over as the fury engulfed him, and he knew he should stop it in order to preserve his strength for whatever lay ahead, but he would not let himself. Finally, after what might have been minutes or maybe even hours, he did began to quiet the movement, but not the thought that lay behind it.

Hang on. Yes, somehow he had to hang on. He had to find out what all this was about. But how? He was powerless. Here he was, God only knew where, bound and gagged and blindfolded. What could he do? What could he — ?

"...has Panther changed the orders...?"

Again, Nate shook his head vigorously, trying to clear it. There they were again, the strange thoughts. But somehow they seemed different this time. Not thoughts. No, more like...conversation. He was hearing someone speak, but not with his ears. He was hearing the conversation inside his head.

Christ! He really was going crazy. He had to stop it. He had to get his mind under control. He —

"...direct line? I just follow orders, like you?"

"But why didn't we finish him off already? Why don't we just get rid of him, like the others?"

"No. We can't. Not yet. There's something special about this one. Panther wants to interrogate him personally. Then, we'll get rid of him, too."

"I hope you're right..."

"They" were talking about him! Nate knew it. He had to get out of here. But he didn't even know where "here" was. And even if he did, so what? What chance did he have of escaping when he couldn't even put his hands in front of himself?

"...here soon?"

"Listen, I don't know any more about this than you do. Panther will be here when he gets here. Why the fuck are you so uptight, anyway? I've never seen anything get to you like this."

"Yeah, I guess you're right. I can't understand it myself. There's just something about that kid that makes me nervous. There's something funny going on, and I can't put my finger on it."

"Ah, come on, relax. What's to worry about now? The snatch is over. We brought him in without even so much as a whimper."

"I know. Maybe that's what it is. I don't like it when something comes off too easy. It makes me suspicious."

"Of what?"

"Don't know. Just suspicious."

"Okay. I see your point. But it can't be long. Panther's been notified. He's on his way over. He'll be here any time. And when he's through with the punk, we'll be able to finish the job."

Finish? That meant kill! And it didn't sound like it was too far off. He had to escape. Somehow.

No, wait! Even if he did get away from these hoodlums, he would still be no better off than before. He wouldn't know who they were or why they were trying to destroy him. No, he had to face this this "Panther" if he wanted to get any answers.

But that was no good, either. So what if he got all the answers and wound up being killed in the end? What good would that do?

There had to be some middle ground, some way of finding out what he wanted to know without putting his life on the line.

His back began to itch between his shoulder blades, and it served as a reminder of how ridiculous his thinking had been. He sat back down on the sofa and wiggled around trying to relieve the discomfort, but with little success. Damn! If he couldn't even scratch his own back, what chance did he have of coming out of this thing alive?

Finally, he stretched out again and tried once more to get some sleep. But the clutter in his mind wouldn't let him —

"What was that call about?"

"Panther. He'll be here in about five minutes. He wants us to get him ready?"

"Yeah. Guess we better do it then. But tell me something, Otter. How long you been with Control?"

"You know we're not supposed to talk about personnel information."

"Sure, I know it. But it's just this: I've been an agency man for nearly a decade, and this is the weirdest operation I've ever been involved in. How about you?"

"What I think is that you're letting your imagination get the best of you. I think you should take a little furlough when we finish this assignment. Get away from things. Maybe go over to the Alps and do some skiing."

"Look, I'm alright. Honest, I am. There's just something about this kid that bothers me."

"Okay, so relax. Let's go get the boy. It can't be much longer till we'll have him out of our hair."

Nate felt the sweat begin to drip off his face, and he drew himself up in a convulsive shiver. Then, slowly, he let himself sit up. But, as he did so, he felt a pounding inside his head.

Not now! He had to have all his wits about him, now. He *couldn't* have one of those headaches.

There was a noise outside of the room, and he knew they had arrived to take him away.

He stood and clenched his fists together, his fingernails again biting into his palms. The headache was intensifying. His upper arm muscles began to quiver as his anger mounted. No, this couldn't be happening, now. Not now! The top of his head felt like it was about to pop off.

But, somehow, over the rumble inside his skull, he heard a key being inserted into the door.

"They" were out there, but soon they would be in here. They were going to take him to his doom. He *couldn't* let that happen!

No, he had to — *had to* let it happen. He had to have answers. Only there must be some other way. There must be —

Kidder!

Of course! Somehow, Kidder fit into this. That son-of-a-bitch had sold him down the river, but Kidder might be his salvation. McBride might be able to give him the answers he needed so he could fit this puzzle together without facing this "Panther."

His ears picked up the sound of the doorknob turning as the hammers began to chip away at bits and pieces of his skull. It seemed almost a miracle that he could hear something like that through all the clamor inside his head, but he did.

He knew it was an insane thought, but he couldn't stop himself from thinking it: *Now, he could "afford" to escape.* Now, he wouldn't have to wait around to see "Panther" to get his answers.

The door began to creak open as Nate flexed his muscles, and he felt the handcuffs snap.

"Damn!" he heard someone shout as his hand came around to jerk the blindfold away from his eyes.

But he never made it. He felt the pain inside his head mushroom into a bomb.

INTERLUDE H

"What do you mean, he's gone? I thought your men had him in a secure holding area?"

"They did, or at least I thought they did. But when I arrived, he had escaped."

"Escaped? How? Wasn't he being held under maximum restraint?"

"Those were my orders, and my men swear they had been carried out to the letter. Apparently, he broke free of his handcuffs and bolted out of the cell before they could stop him."

"Panther, I'm quite surprised at you. You should know better than to send novices out on an assignment as sensitive as this one? Certain measures — "

"Sir! Both these men have been CONTROL operatives for years. And he was cuffed with high-test super alloy tungsten. But he shattered it as though it were paper.

"Good Lord! If he has the mental ability to do feats of that magnitude, he's much more of a threat than any of the others were. There's no question about it — he must be destroyed soon!"

"Sir, I agree completely. There's just one problem."

"What's that?"

"First, we have to find him again."

"Yes...yes.... Then, maybe what you need is some good bait."

CHAPTER FIFTEEN

Nate felt his own lumpy mattress beneath him. There could be no mistaking it. He knew every one of those lumps personally. This bed had seen many nights of ecstasy. He and Casta had —

Casta! But Casta was gone.

And now he was alone in this bed.

But what was he doing here?

He opened his eyes and let his gaze slowly wander around the room. But it didn't wander far.

"Hi."

She was sitting in a chair — one of his kitchen chairs — staring at him, smiling. Though it hadn't been the smile or the chair which had grabbed his attention. It was her *body*. Her *great* body. Her great, *nude* body!

"Hello," he tried to reply. He wasn't sure if it came out that way, but some kind of sound issued from his throat.

"You look so cute lying there, I just had to watch you."

"Oh, I see." Actually, he didn't. Who was she and what was she doing here? What was *he* doing here, for that matter?

She nodded, and her smile broadened. Those tits and those legs. He couldn't take his eyes off them. He knew he'd seen her before somewhere.

"Been sitting there long?"

"No, not long. About a half hour — ever since I got up."

Got up? Did that mean he'd been sleeping with this gorgeous creature? No, not sleeping. Surely not sleeping.

"What time is it?" he asked, and maybe he should have added, "What day?" but he didn't.

"Nearly noon."

"Noon!"

"Yeah. Why? You planning on going someplace?"

"No, not really." Nowhere but the nearest insane asylum.

"Good, 'cause I was figuring on fixing you something to eat. Got lots of food in the cabinets. You just stock up?"

"Yeah, Cass just went — uh, that is, I just went to the grocery." Who was she? That brown hair, blue eyes, and the smile all looked so familiar.

"What you like?"

"Huh?"

"What do you want me to fix you?"

"Oh, anything'll be fine."

"Uh-unh. If I'd wanted to fix 'anything,' I could've done it already. Now, you tell me."

She stood, and he got his first full view of her lower body area. Christ! That luscious brown hair around it almost glistened.

Slowly, she strolled over toward him, grinning all the way.

That walk! He knew he'd seen it before. At...at — at the library! After he and Casta had quarreled over his physical readiness to attend classes. She'd been the one who'd dropped her pencil.

Her tongue curled out of her mouth as she reached him, and she bent over and tickled his lips with it. He closed his eyes and tasted it. Delicious.

She slipped down and sat on the edge of the bed, continuing their embrace. After more than a minute, she broke it. "Well, move over, silly."

He obliged, and she slipped her smooth, creamy skin next to his dark tan body, which, he discovered, was likewise completely naked. She ran her fingers through his hair as her lips moved about his face. Her tongue did a dance of delight around his ears as it moved on down to his neck, then his chest, and further downward. Then, he could feel her warm, moist lips around him, vibrating excitement throughout his body.

As she continued to embrace him, he ran his fingers through her hair, feeling each silky strand. Finally, with a little effort, he disengaged her and dragged her face toward his. Their lips pressed together, he rolled her over onto her back and entered her. She was hot, throbbing, almost like riding a wild pony — one that couldn't stay mounted for long. Sure enough, it was over very soon, and Nate found himself lying exhausted crosswise in the bed.

After a few seconds, she sat up and looked into his eyes.

"That wasn't what I was talking about when I asked you what you wanted."

Nate tried to smile, but he wasn't sure he mastered it. "Eggs. I like eggs."

"That's not enough."

"Scrambled. Scrambled will be fine." Really, he would have preferred an omelet. Casta would have made him an omelet.

Casta! Dead only a few days and already he was doing this in the bed they'd shared. And with a strange, white girl, at that.

Oh, Casta, Casta. How long had she been dead? Was she already buried? Probably. And he hadn't even been present at her funeral. What did her parents think of him? Some bastard who used their daughter for screwing but didn't give a damn about her memory!

"That's not true!" he shouted.

"What?" The brown-haired beauty had been about to leave the bedroom. Now, she turned to face him again. "What's not true?"

"Oh...nothing. It's nothing." The hell it was nothing. It was everything to him. Casta had been his whole life, and now she was gone. She was gone, and here he was lying to some white girl he couldn't even remember picking up, saying that Casta was nothing.

He could feel moisture on his cheeks, but before he could raise a hand to wipe away the tears, she was already pulling his face toward her body and squeezing it between her breasts.

"Tell me about it. I'll listen," she offered.

Listen? Yes, he needed someone to listen.

"I...I can't." Could he trust her? "I don't know where to begin."

"Just — "

"About last night," he asked, wiping away the last of his tears and pulling away from her, "What happened? Tell me about it. I...don't remember."

"Well, I would really be surprised if you did. I found you down on Coleman Street sauntering along in a daze. I recognized you from school and figured you must be out on some pretty hard stuff. I tried to talk with you, but you just kept on mumbling something about "getting to the controls," or something like that. What does that mean? Does it mean *anything*?"

Nate shook his head, but he knew it meant something, only he didn't know what.

"Then you started saying you had to get 'back to McBride's.' But when I took you to McBride's, after one drink you were ready to go again."

"McBride's?" Of course, Kidder's!

"Sure. I figured you must go there a lot. I had heard of the place, but — pardon me — I didn't think much of it. "I've been to a lot more exciting bars in my time. Anyway, I figured I better get you home before you passed out on me, but I had a devil of a time getting you to tell me your address. And then, when we got here, you started screaming about the 'cream-colored car.' That mean anything?"

Nate shook his head again. Lying seemed to have become a habit with him lately, though maybe it wasn't really lying when you didn't know what something meant. His mind slipped back to the last time he'd been in his apartment before — to the fight with Lacy.

"Tell me something: What kind of condition was this place in when you — we — got here?" he asked.

"What'sa matter? You got housewife mentality?"

"No. Just tell me."

"It was spotless."

"It was? Then, how 'bout the door? Was it locked?"

"Well, no — "

"But the apartment itself was all straightened up?"

"As I said: 'spotless.' Why you so worried about that? I've been to guy's apartments knee-deep in beer cans. Don't bother me."

"I see." Evidently Lacy or somebody in his bunch had cleaned up the place — probably after they searched it thoroughly. But for what?

"Hey, you gonna tell me what's bugging you?" she asked.

"Huh? Oh, it's nothing. I'm alright. See." He presented his teeth in a false smile.

"Sure you are, and I'm the Mata Hari."

"You are?"

"Hell, you know what I mean, Kidder."

"What did you call me?"

"Kidder. You said that's your name. But I guess it

ain't your real handle, is it?"

"No...it's not. When did I tell you to call me Kidder?"

"Well, you didn't exactly say, `Call me Kidder.' It was when I found you and you were begging me to take you to McBride's."

"Figures."

"What?"

"Oh, never mind."

"Listen, Kidder — "

"The name's Nate, Nathan Tibbetts."

"Nate. I like that. But why do they call you Kidder? You a big joker, or something?"

"They don't."

"They don't what?"

"They don't call me 'Kidder.'"

"Then, why did you tell me — ?"

"Listen, it's a long story, but let's just drop it, okay!"

"Anything you say, uh, uh..."

"Nate."

"Sure, Nate." She stood up again.

"Listen, I'm sorry. I didn't mean to sound ungrateful. It's just that I've been through a lot lately."

"I gathered that."

"Anyway, thanks for taking care of me."

"Sure, Nate, it was *my* pleasure. It *really* was. When we got inside here last night, you started begging me to stay, and I'm *glad* I did. We jumped in the sack, and I had the best time ever. And I mean it."

"You're not going to give me that line about black studs, are you?"

"Hell, no. You're not the first African-American guy I've been to bed with. But I can tell you this: You made me feel better than anybody I've ever been with before. Not only did you know how to pour it on, but you made me feel like I was important as a person, too. And, believe me, I know that's hard" — She grinned broadly, adding, "no pun intended — especially on a one-night stand. Most guys don't even try. And, really, I don't usually care how much the guy's getting out of it, as long as I get my kicks. But last night with you was different."

She bent down and kissed him again briefly.

"Thanks."

"No, thank you, Nate, for a very special time. And I know something's bothering you. I don't know what, but when you get ready to talk about it, I'll be ready to listen."

She stepped into the bathroom. A couple minutes later, he heard the toilet flush, and she came out, dressed in a pair of navy-blue slacks and a flowered blouse.

"Thought I'd better get into my clothes before I start cooking. Don't want to splatter grease on my naked body," she said, smiling again.

"No, you wouldn't want to do that."

She was almost out of the room when he stopped her again.

"Hey, what did you say your name is?" he asked.

"Never did," she called from the living room, as she made her way toward the kitchen. "You never asked, and I never volunteered. Most ungentlemanly of you."

He jumped up and slipped on the dirty suit pants he'd been wearing. At the kitchen doorway a moment later, he continued the interrupted conversation.

"Hell, woman, are you gonna tell me or not?"

She closed the refrigerator door, two eggs in each hand, and grinning broadly. "Tell you what?"

"You know good and well what I mean: Your name? What's your name, dammit?"

"Oh, that...It's Sandy. Actually, it's Sandra. Sandra Aarons."

"See there, now. That wasn't so bad, was it?" he

asked, smiling himself.

"No, it's just that it's usually the *first* thing a guy asks me, right before he gets around to inquiring about my phone number. Which really means: 'Can I call you up and take you out, then bring you back and screw you?'"

"Quite the cynic, aren't you?"

"I've met enough guys in my time to know what they're after."

"And what *you're* after? Isn't it why you were cruising Coleman? You were looking for some guy to screw!"

Why was he talking this way to this woman who had found him wandering around and helped him? Perhaps *he* was the cynic, after all.

Sandy put the two eggs down beside the sink, her smile now gone. But she nodded.

"Yeah," she said, finally. "The knife cuts both ways. I was out cruising for some action. I was horny, and you looked like a good prospect. But what I told you a few minutes ago, that wasn't just a line. I really meant it."

She picked up the eggs again and started to break them into the skillet she had placed on the stove, then she glanced back over at him. "Oh, you want some bacon, too? I better fry that first, if you do."

"Listen, uh...Sandy, I can fix the food. You're my guest here. I should be cookin' for you. I'm not into that sexist bag."

"Well, neither am I, but I like to cook. I really do. Now, do you want bacon to go with your eggs, or not?"

"That would be great. You think I got time for a quick shower while it's cookin'?"

"Sure, go ahead. But you really like bathing, don't you?"

"Why?"

"Cause you insisted on taking a shower last night before you would go to bed."

"I did?"

"You did."

"Maybe I'll skip it, then. I'll just get dressed in some *clean* clothes.

Back in the bedroom, he selected a fresh-smelling, but faded pair of blue jeans and a brown-and-white stripped shirt. It was one Casta had given him. When he'd come across the shirt, he'd tried to ignore it, even though it had always been one of his favorites. There were just too many memories. Finally, he decided he wasn't acting reasonably, grabbing the shirt and pulling it on quickly. Also, he found money in a drawer where Casta always "stashed" it and pocketed the eighty-seven dollars.

By the time he returned to the kitchen, he found Sandy already setting the table.

"Hope you like it crispy," she said, serving him bacon.

"That's fine." But his mind wasn't really on food.

She slid into a chair across from him. "I'm here; yoo-hoo. You've got that far-away look again."

"Oh, do I? Hey, what day is it, anyway?"

"What day? Sunday, of course. You think I could goof around with you like this on a week day?"

"No, I guess not."

"Why?"

Why? Because he was trying to remember what day Casta had been killed and this whole mad trip had started. But he couldn't. It was all clouds and mist. No substance. It had all happened a hundred years ago, maybe — or in another lifetime.

"Oh, no reason," he responded at last. "I've just lost track of the days." And months and years and his life and everything!

He heard the sound of an automobile roaring by outside, and it took him back to the last evening he'd spent in his apartment — after his world had been destroyed by a heavy metal awning. He had thought he didn't care to go on living for a few seconds afterward, but he'd been mistaken. He'd known that for a long time, now. He had to go on for at least long enough to find out why Casta had been murdered — why she had died in his stead.

But more than why. He had to pay them back. He had to find those responsible and punish them for what they'd done to her — and him. At last, he realized, he had a place to start. Those final few seconds he could remember before waking up here came back to him. And he knew he had to return to Kidder's house. He *had* to go back — but this time not to hide out. This time he would be going there to start putting the puzzle together.

"Excuse me," he mumbled, standing up and knocking over his chair in the process.

Less than a minute later, he was running out the front door of his apartment building.

CHAPTER SIXTEEN

The cab driver had given up his effort to make conversation, with Nate hardly bothering even to respond to his questions. As the vehicle made its way through the neighborhood in which he had spent most of his life, Nate couldn't help remembering those cheerful boyhood days spent with Kidder.

"The bastard," he whispered.

"What?" the cabbie asked.

"Nothing," he responded.

"Sure, fellow, 'nothing,'" the cabbie countered.

Maybe it was nothing now, but it had been something once. A team — that's what they'd been.

Outside his vehicle, he could see men and women and kids, too, all dressed in their finery. Returning from church. Oblivious to his pain — to his mission. Which was? What was his mission? One step at a time. That was the way he'd take it. Right now, he'd concentrate just on Kidder. He'd find out what this thing was about, then he would have plenty of time to worry about what to do next. Or would he?

Was he doing the right thing coming back here? What if the whole gang was waiting for him? He couldn't hope to escape again. That would be too much luck to wish for.

Escape? Yes, he had escaped from the two men in ski masks. But how? It was all very fuzzy. He tried to concentrate on it, but he couldn't. They had taken him somewhere, but he couldn't remember where or how he had gotten away. He couldn't remember a lot of things lately.

As it turned onto Whitney Boulevard, the taxi slowed, and Nate knew the driver was looking for house numbers — for Kidder's house number. It was in the next block. He could have told the man that, but he didn't feel like it.

"Stop!" he shouted, and the driver hit the brake. Nate grabbed the door handle and began to lift up. "How much?"

The driver read the meter and told him the charge, then added: "But it's still more than a block to the address you said you wanted."

"This is fine." He didn't feel like arguing with the cabbie. He threw the money at him and leaped out of the vehicle. Then, he stood on the sidewalk and waited for the taxi to drive away. When it was out of sight, he began to slowly make his way toward Kidder's.

No use taking chances, he told himself. As if he wasn't taking a chance in simply coming back here. But, at least, he wouldn't be riding up in a cab, which Kidder would spot even before he got out and call the others again.

Nate spied Kidder's car in the driveway more than a half-block away. But he saw no sign of activity. Maybe Kidder, Clarice, and Tyrone were all inside.

They were. Eating lunch. Nate watched them for more than a minute through a side window before he moved around to the front of the house. On the rotting old front porch, a board creaked, but not loudly, and a few seconds later he threw open the front door.

"Don't nobody get up!" he shouted.

They all stared at the man standing in their doorway. Nate slammed the door behind him and marched resolutely over to the table.

"Uh...uh...have a seat, Tibman," Kidder stammered.

"No, *thank you*," he responded through gritted teeth. Out of the corner of his eyes, he could see Clarice's mouth sag open.

"Nate, what is it?" she asked, finally. But Nate's focus did not leave Kidder's eyes.

"Shut up, woman. Let me handle this!" her husband shouted. Then to Nate: "How 'bout some chicken?" Kidder held out a bowl with a drumstick and a wing. Nate pushed it away.

"Don't start that *shit*."

"'Kay, Tibman. Just tryin' to be neighborly."

"Like you were last night, I'll bet!"

"Last night?"

"Hell, yeah, last night, when I was here."

"But that was — "

"Dammit, man, I didn't come here to argue over what day it was. I come here for answers. And I'm gonna get 'em."

"Sure, Tibman. But I don't know none."

"Don't gimme *that* shit, either."

"Honest, Tibman, I — "

Nate's right hand shot out and grabbed the other man by the shirt collar, lifting him from his chair. He heard a scream, and he glanced over at the woman, who stifled the sound almost immediately.

"Answers, I said," Nate continued, jerking Kidder away from the table and throwing him to the floor. He heard another whimper, then someone began to cry, but he knew it wasn't Clarice this time. It had the ring of an infant's voice.

"Daddy, daddy!" the child bellowed.

"Sh-h-h-h, honey," he heard the woman say, trying to reassure her son. "It'll be all right. Why don't me and you go in th' bedroom 'n' play?"

Nate looked her squarely in the eyes. "No! Nobody leaves this room."

"But Tyrone's scared — " she began.

"Dammit, don't you see, I don't really give a fuck! Now sit back down. You, too!" He pointed toward Kidder, who began to raise himself off the floor. A few seconds later, he was again sitting in the dining chair.

"Now, Kidder, I told you I wanted answers — "

"But I don't know nothin'. Honest, Tibman. I swear it."

"You think I'd believe that after what happened to me last — hell, the last time I'ze here?"

"But — "

"Why have people been tryin' to kill me?"

"Tibman, I told you — "

Nate delivered a backhand across Kidder's cheek. The child screamed, and he heard the woman begin to whimper.

"'Why?' I said."

"I don't — "

"Alright, let's try somethin' dif'rent. How 'bout tellin' me who th' goons were who took me away from here?"

"Tibman, I — "

Nate grabbed the other by his collar again and shook him vigorously. "Are you gonna tell me what I wanta know, or am I gonna haveta beat you to death with my bare hands?"

"No, Nate, stop, please. Can't you see — ?" But Clarice fell silent when he looked around, into her eyes. The child was still whimpering.

"'Kay, Tibman, I'll tell ever'thin' I know, but ain't much. Then, will you leave me alone?"

"No promises, you lyin' ass son-of-a-bitch. Just start talkin'."

Kidder's eyes shifted in his wife's direction, then back to Nate's. "They come over th' other night, 'fore you did.

They said they'd kill Clarice 'n' th' baby if I didn't cooperate. I didn't have no choice, don't you see? I couldn't let 'em kill my family, could I?"

Nate offered no comment, so after a few seconds of silence, Kidder continued.

"They said if you showed up to get you to go to bed and call 'em when you went to sleep, and I better let 'em know 'bout it right away — or they'd get my wife and young'un. They woulda done it, too. I know they woulda, Tibman. They wudn't kiddin'. I could see it in their eyes."

Another pause.

"So?" Nate asked "Go on."

"That's all, Tibman. There ain't no more. I don't know nothin' else."

Nate clenched his teeth, and his eyes became mere slits.

"No!" he screamed, and launched himself toward Kidder.

The chair shattered as he landed on top of the other man, and the two of them went crashing to the floor. He threw a rapid combination of fists against the other's body and face before he felt an arm around his neck, tugging back on him.

He realized suddenly that both the woman and the child were screeching at the tops of their lungs.

"No, no, no!" Clarice screamed, as she tried to pull him off her husband. "Stop, Nate. Please, stop. Please!"

Finally, exhausted, he fell off the other man's chest onto the hard wood floor and began to cry himself.

"It's not fair!" he whimpered. "I've got to know. I've got to know."

He looked over at the woman, now trying to wipe the blood off her husband's face with the tail of her Sunday dress.

"Don't you see? I've got to find out. Somebody's tryin'

to kill me. Like I told you before, they already killed Cass. If I don't find out who it is, they gonna get me, soon. Got no place to go."

Kidder had begun to sit up, with the help of his wife, and he looked over at Nate who was still sprawled on the floor.

"That's why I come here, Kidder. I didn't know no other place to go," he said, now directing his words-mixed-with-tears toward the other man.

Clarice gave him a look filled with hatred, as she tried to pull her husband to his feet, but Kidder pushed her away and knelt beside Nate.

"Brother, I didn't want to do it, don't you see? I was just scared, that's all. Scared for my woman 'n' baby. I didn't know what else to do, don't you see?"

Nate tried to calm himself as Kidder's hand went out to grasp his.

"You got thunder in them fists, bro. I think maybe you missed your callin'," Kidder continued. "Here, let me help you up."

With Kidder's hand clasped around his arm, the two of them stood, and the other directed them toward the living room. Both sank onto the worn-out sofa.

"Them's some bad dudes, bro," Kidder added.

Nate nodded.

"And like I said, I don't know no more, but I can guess, if you want me to." Kidder held out both hands, palms up.

"Be more than I can do."

"Then I 'spect they're gov'ment."

"Cops?"

"Not just cops. More like the FBI or something like that maybe. They just seemed like big-time gov'ment men to me."

"Why would the FBI be after me?"

"You been into any big deals lately, bro?"

"Deals? You mean drugs? Come on, Kidder. You know me better'n that."

"I useta know you, Tibman. But I ain't seen you much since school. I don't know what you been into lately."

"Nothin' like that. I'm just tryin' to finish up my schoolin', that's all."

"'Kay, bro, I believe you. But somebody must think you're into something, else why would they want you so bad?"

"And why would they want me dead?"

"Beats me, brother."

Clarice had come into the room, holding Tryone, and the two of them sat in a chair, listening to the conversation. The look of hatred had melted some, having been replaced with one more of disgust or anger, perhaps, Nate wasn't sure which.

"Kidder, I tell you: They been tryin' to kill me. These dudes mean business, comin' in here and takin' me away in handcuffs and a blindfold — "

"How *did you* get away from 'em?"

"Escaped. I escaped."

"I figured that, or you wouldn't be here, now. But how did you do it?"

"I, uh...they, uh... Well, I was locked up somewhere, and I heard 'em talkin' about killin' me, so I knew I had to get away. When they unlocked the door, I made a break for it."

"And they didn't try to stop you?"

"No, I guess they were pretty shook up after I...I broke... their handcuffs."

"You what?"

"Listen, Kidder, it's all kinda hazy, but I have this memory of breakin' th' handcuffs right off my wrists."

Kidder stared wide-eyed, unspeaking.

"But that can't be right, can it? You can't just break handcuffs."

The other shrugged, then added: "You sure got powerful fists, but I don't 'spect you're strong 'nough to break outa handcuffs. You sure it happened that way?"

"No. I told you it was hazy. Can't remember. I just can't." He put his hands to his temples and rubbed them vigorously.

"Maybe they wudn't locked good or somethin'," Kidder offered, after a moment of silence. Nate looked up. "What?"

"Maybe they didn't have the cuffs locked completely, you think maybe?"

"Could be. Anything could be." Nate stood up. "Nothin' makes sense anymore. I just can't figure why they're out to get me."

Kidder stood, too. He took a step toward Nate and placed a hand on his back. "I'm sorry 'bout this whole thing, Tibman. You know I wouldn't a done it if it hadn't been — "

Nate turned and waved a hand in the other's face. "It's over now. Don't worry 'bout it."

He looked into Kidder's eyes, and he saw honesty there, honesty and compassion. But he also saw a battered face, a face that he had battered.

"Kidder, look, what can I say? This thing's about drove me nuts. I can't figure nothing out. And now I come in here and about half kill you. I never wanted...I never meant to..."

"Like you said: 'sover. Forget it."

Nate glanced at Clarice and Tyrone, and he saw that some of the anger had even gone out of her face, too. But he suspected it would be a long time before she could ever completely forgive him for what he'd done today.

"I better be gettin' outa here," he offered.

"You sure you won't stay for dinner? We got plenty left."

"No. Just had breakfast before I came over. Besides, they may be watching here or be on my tail. Can't hang around in one place too long. Just wish I knew — "

"Wait a minute!" Kidder said in a half shout. "I just 'membered somethin' I heard one of 'em mumble."

"What?"

"Don't make no sense, 'specially since your mama's name is Sara."

"Come on — out with it, man!"

"Th' dude said somethin' 'bout you bein' th' last a Dinah's kids."

"Dinah's kids?"

"Yeah, that's what he said."

"Dinah's kids? Why would he say something like that?"

"Probably just got your mama's name wrong."

Nate let himself drop back onto the old sofa, shaking his head.

"Told you it was nothin'," Kidder added.

There was silence for a few seconds, then Nate slipped the forefinger of his right hand up to his lips and began tapping them gently as he spoke again. "No, it means something. It must mean something."

"But what?"

Again, Nate shook his head. "I don't — wait! I just remembered something. Mama — yeah, that must be it! But what does *that* mean?"

"What're you talkin' 'bout, Tibman?"

Nate turned to stare into Kidder's eyes. "Not Dinah. It was dinosaur. The last time I saw her, Mama called herself an old *dinosaur!*"

INTERLUDE I

"If he begins to piece things together, it could prove more than disastrous. We cannot permit the existence of CONTROL to become known now or ever! Do I make myself clear?"

"Perfectly, sir!"

"Good. I remember that there was a time when no one ever got away from the wily Panther before you pounced."

"Those were different times — "

"True. But perhaps you've gone soft with all this routine surveillance."

" — and back then it was a simple matter of excising the problem. And I was dealing with ordinary men. But there's nothing ordinary about Nathan Tibbetts."

"Again, true."

"I'll just be extremely happy to have this matter put behind me once and for all."

"We all will, Panther. I can assure you of that. But now, to the question at hand. There are others in Washington who do not share my confidence or have my patience. Your report, please!"

"Right. I'm afraid that although we anticipated his move, we were too late to apprehend him at his friend's home. Nevertheless, I can report with confidence that we know precisely where he's headed, and we should be able to take him without any trouble, there."

"*I hope so, Panther, for your sake. Where exactly do you expect to find him this time?*"

"*At the hospital.*"

CHAPTER SEVENTEEN

"Mama?"

"Sonny! I thought you wudn't never comin' back."

He stepped over to the hospital bed and hugged her. "Let me look at you," he said, standing back a bit. "You're lookin' better." Liar! She looked awful. Her eyes had sunken in. She was skinnier than ever.

"Boy, didn't I always teach you to tell th' truth."

"Yes'm."

"Then don't go fibbin' to your Mama."

"But, Mama — "

"No, buts. I thought you tole me you'as gonna come by and see me ever day."

"I did, Mama. I'm sorry."

"Don't you think a mama wants to see her boy?"

He nodded. "I know I shoulda — "

"Does it bother you comin' to this place? What is it, Sonny?"

Should he tell her? No, he couldn't tell her what had been happening, not with her in this shape. But he should say something so she wouldn't think he was simply an ingrate.

"It's Casta, Mama — "

"Yeah, didn't I tell you to bring her along next time."

"Uh-huh, you told me that, but — "

"Then, why didn't you, boy?" She struggled to sit up a little, then fell back onto her pillow.

"I couldn't, Mama."

"And why not? You didn't want her to see me layin' here like this?"

"No, Mama, nothing like that."

"Then what is it?"

"If you'll just hush up for a second, I'll tell you."

She already had her mouth open to offer a retort, but she let it close, without comment.

"Casta is..." And he felt that lump in his throat as big as a baseball. "Well, Mama, Casta's dead, that's what!"

"She's what?"

"Yeah, she's dead. That's why I haven't been around in a while."

"What happened, Sonny? Tell me about it." He could see the tears in her sunken eye sockets fighting their way to get out.

"It was...an accident. We went to a show, and when we were leaving, the awning fell on her."

"Th' what?"

"The awning — the little roof outside the theater. It crushed her. She died instantly, I think. No suffering."

"Oh, Sonny. I'm so sorry I been so hard on you, boy." She held out both arms, and he came to her and weeped in great, heaving sobs on her breast.

"I tried to save her, Mama, but there was nothing I could do. Honest, Mama." And someday somebody would pay for it, too. Maybe thanks to some answers she would give him today. But not just yet. Not yet, because he couldn't stop the tears yet.

"Hush, hush, boy. It'll be alright."

"How, Mama? How can it be alright? Cass is gone. I'll never see her again."

"I know 'bout that stuff, Sonny. 'Member?"

Yes, if anyone did, Mama did..

"You never really get over it," she continued. "But finally you learn to accept it. When your Daddy got killed over in Iraq, at first I refused to b'lieve it was him. Even after they sent his body back home, I tried to pretend there'd been some terrible mistake, that th' man in th' coffin wudn't really your daddy, that he was jus' his double, somebody who looked jus' like him, only wudn't him. I pretended that any day your daddy would walk through the front door.... 'Course he never did."

With a feeble hand under his chin, she raised his head so his eyes were focused on hers.

"Just haveta accept it and go on. It hurts. It'll hurt you prob'ly th' resta your life, but accept it."

He sniffed and raised himself off her, slumping into a chair beside the bed. Both were silent for several minutes.

Finally, looking out the window, she began again, this time on a different subject.

"Doctors say maybe I can go home pretty soon, Sonny."

What? He couldn't believe what he was hearing.

She didn't look his way, but kept right on speaking. "I can go home 'bout any time — if I want to. You think I should? What you think? Should I?"

Despite everything that had happened in his life in the last few days — despite everything that was still happening — he found himself smiling. "Sure, Mama. That sounds great!"

But his joy was short-lived. She looked over at him, her face a picture of sorrow. "I know what they're tellin' me. They're sayin' I can go home to die."

His own smile disappeared, and he found himself sinking into a deeper pit of depression than he had been in before. "No, Mama. That's not it."

The hell it wasn't! Here he was lying to her again.

"You don't think I'm stupid as well as sick, do you, Sonny? I know what it means."

"Mama, please." He had to change the subject, to get

her mind off it.

"Reckon how much longer I got? Six months? A year?"

Oh, if only it was a year. He would cherish that year — make it the best year of her life.

"Mama, you remember when I was in here last time?"

"...Can't be very long. I just ain't doin' no good. Maybe two years at the most. What you think?"

"About that last time — "

"...Did Dr. Dryden tell you how long I got?"

"Are you listening to me?"

"Well, did he, Sonny?" Shit, she wasn't going to stop until he gave her some kind of answer, but not the truth. How could he tell her she would be dead in a few weeks or less?

"Yes, Mama, you got cancer. That's what your doctor told me. He also said that almost half of all cancer can be cured. It'll take a while — "

"Sonny, Sonny, don't gimme that. They ain't tryin' to cure me."

"Maybe they're getting ready to start."

"No, they ain't. If they was gonna do it, they woulda already started. I ain't stupid."

"But — "

"All I want from you is *the truth,* boy! How long have I got?"

"Okay, okay. A while. They can't be certain."

"How long?"

"These things are hard to pin down exactly."

She bolted upright and shouted: "*How long? I have a right to know. It's my life!*"

"A few weeks, maybe less."

Oh, my God, he'd told her. He'd actually told her.

She let her weak frame settle back onto the bed. "Thank you, Sonny. I needed to know that. I ain't afraid a dyin', you know, boy. I jus' wanted to know how much longer I got to spend with you. You're all I got left, you know."

He fell back onto her breast, sobbing again, this time for the other woman in his life, who was also about to be taken away.

"Hush, hush. Now, don't you cry for me, Sonny. I'm ready to meet my Maker. Th' onliest thing I regret is havin' to leave you behind."

"Oh, Mama!"

The tears didn't stop easily this time, not when he was crying for two.

Then, he remembered the third — himself. He might soon be the next one to go. He managed finally to choke back his emotions.

"Last time I was here, Mama, you called yourself a 'dinosaur.' What did you mean?" he asked, raising himself off her a second time.

"Oh, that? I was talkin' 'bout the ol' Dinosaur Project."

"Dinosaur Project? Is that an old housing project or something?"

"It was *somethin'* alright, but it wudn't no housing project. You 'member me tellin' you how me and your daddy took part in this science study one time?"

"You mean the cancer research project?"

"Yeah, that's it. Dr. Gamov's project, only all a us called it the Dinosaur Project."

"You did? Why?"

She took her right hand and ran it through his coal-black hair. "I don't rightly know. It was jus' th' name it was called by."

"Kinda making fun of it?"

She shook her head slightly. "Don't think so. Even Dr. Gamov called it that hisself sometimes, so I guess that was the real name of it for some reason, but I don't know why."

"Oh. Thanks, Mama."

"Why you want to know 'bout Dinosaur?"

"Uh, uh, no reason. I just remembered you saying that before and wondered what you meant?"

"Yeah?"

"Yeah!"

"That ain't all. Don't fib to me again, boy. I can tell when you're doin' it."

Damn! How was he going to get out of this one without worrying her more?

"Well, I'm waitin'."

"It was about that research, Mama. I, uh, just wanted to see what was involved in it — to see if there was anything there to help you."

"No. Don't bother. Dr. Gamov gave up on it twenty years ago."

"Well, how did you get involved? And why?"

"Why? That's simple: money. They paid us two hundred dollars a day. Back then, wudn't no other place a black person could make that kinda money. Not 'less you had a education."

"I guess not."

"Was dif'rent back then, you know. We just had to take what we could get. Your daddy and me — we was still goin' together then. It was before we got married. They wanted young people, even younger than you are now, you see — well, we was lucky to get this. A lots wanted it, but not many was picked. Maybe 'bout ten or twelve of us, I 'spect."

"Was everyone African-American who took part in these tests."

"Uh-huh. Only we was all 'black' in them days. Some of us still called ourselves 'colored.'" She smiled slightly.

"And where did these tests take place?"

"Where? Why, where you are, a course."

"Where?"

"At the *university*."

"Sure, that makes sense," he said, shrugging and standing up at the some time. "Well, I suspect I better be running along and let you get some rest. The nurses jump on me if I stick around too long."

She reached out and grabbed his left hand in her right. "Don't pay them no mind, Sonny."

He stooped and hugged her again. Close-up, it was easy to see the exhaustion in her face.

"And thanks for tellin' me th' truth 'bout how long I got. I know it wudn't easy for you."

Standing, he tried to give her a cautious, but optimistic smile.

She released his hand, and he watched as slowly her eyelids creeped shut. He stood watching her for several more minutes as the memories slipped past, memories of a meeting which took place almost a year ago.

"Mama, this is Casta Jordan," he said.

"Well, ain't you th' perty one," Mama said.

Casta extended her right hand. "I'm pleased to meet you, Mrs. Tibbetts. Nate has told me so much about you."

"Call me 'Mama.' If you're gonna marry my boy, you'd better get used to that."

Casta gave Mama her warmest smile. "All right, Mama."

"Well, y'all come on in th' house and I'll get us somethin' to drink."

Mama led the way inside and insisted Casta seat herself in the living room while she got the tea, Casta's favorite drink.

"Sonny — I mean, Nate — told me that, so I stocked up on tea. I really don't drink it much myself. Hope you don't mind me calling your man 'Sonny,' but he's been my boy all these years, and it's kinda a pet name I have for him."

Casta started to laugh. "That's fine, Mrs. Tibbetts — I mean, Mama. I have a pet name for him, too. I call him, 'Tib.' But whether it's 'Sonny,' 'Tib' or 'Nate' doesn't matter so much. What matters is that we both love him."

Mama grabbed Casta and gave her a big hug, and Nate caught the glimmer of a tear in her eyes.

"Chile, we gonna get along jus' fine. I can tell it," Mama said.

That was less than a year ago. Now, Casta was dead, and Mama soon would be.

She had begun to snore lightly by the time Nate came to himself. He knew where he had to go. He had to get back to campus right away. It had been a long time. Twenty years was a considerable span of time for a scientist to stay with one university, but maybe Gamov was still around.

Opening the door to her room, Nate had already placed one foot into the hallway by the time he glimpsed Lacy. Instinctively, he whirled about and zipped back inside his mother's room.

Christ! They'd found him! Again!

He was trapped. There was no way he could get out without being spotted. Then, hide! They would be in the room at any second. He had to find a place to hide.

Frantically, his eyes darted about.

Nowhere.

Nothing.

Wait! — the bathroom. It was the most obvious, but maybe he could get out of sight long enough to think up a plan. He'd escaped once before. Maybe he could do it again — if he only had time to *think*.

He jerked the door open, leaped inside, and slammed it behind himself, punching the lock in. It wasn't much. But he needed time to —

The window!

Hardly realizing what he was doing, he raised the bathroom window and shoved hard against the screen mesh. It easily pulled loose from the rubber edging which held it in place against the metal frame. Climbing first onto the toilet seat, he was able to slip both his right, then his left leg through. His butt proved a problem, however. He was stuck, half-in and half-out! After more than a minute of squirming around, he rested and tried to listen for sounds coming from his mother's room. But he could hear nothing.

What the hell did that prove? Just that he couldn't hear anything — not that they weren't in there.

He felt that obstruction in his throat again, and his palms were all sweaty. Somehow he had to get through this damn window. If they weren't out there now, it wouldn't be much longer.

Twisting his body at a forty-five degree angle and shoving hard finally proved just the ticket. He found himself slipping through. Slowly, he eased his feet out onto the ledge he knew was just outside the window. When he felt a solid foundation underneath him, he let his upper half slip out, too, closing the window behind him.

Don't...look...down. They always told people that in the movies. He knew it was good advice. Babes had said the same thing a few days ago when his rope was breaking. But, as before, he knew he'd never be able to move until he did.

"Shit!"

He threw himself back tightly against the wall. He was really learning to appreciate why they told people that in the movies.

Frozen. His feet were frozen. It was 85 or 90 degrees out here and his feet were "frozen." Somehow, he had to make them move. He had to work his way along this ledge far enough to enter another room and get away before they could catch him. How the hell was he going to do that when he couldn't even...?

Gradually, with extreme concentration, he began to inch his way along the wall. After what seemed like an hour, he allowed himself to glance back in the direction he'd come.

Christ! That wasn't real. It couldn't be right. He wasn't more than five feet from the window where he'd started. How would he ever get away if he didn't move faster?

Nate tried to stop his knees from shaking. How did the stunt guys do it? They had nets, of course. But there was no net below him, only hard concrete. He'd once read that Harold Lloyd actually hung by those clock hands a dozen or so stories up in his famous silent, *Safety Last*, without a thing to catch him. So there must be some secret to it — but what?

Concentrate. He had to think about what he was trying to accomplish and forget about where he was....

No good. How could he forget he was standing on a narrow ledge six stories up?

Move! Just do it. They were probably looking for him all over now. It wouldn't be long before they decided to look out the window. And when they did, it would be "goodbye, Nate." All they had to do was make him lose his balance and everything would be over for him.

With more determination than he thought he could muster, he began to slide along the ledge again. He was still aware that he was six stories up, but somehow his feet worked. He found himself passing another window...and another...and another.

He was just beginning to believe he might make it when *it* struck.

"No!" he whispered to himself. Not that. Anything but that. But there was no mistaking it.

Or stopping it.

The pounding inside his skull was intensifying with every second that passed.

Not now! For God's sake, not now! He clenched his teeth as he felt an angry, convulsive shiver shake his entire body.

Suddenly, he realized that even taking his chances with "them" would be better than taking his chances with this — with what must inevitably follow the headache.

Moving much more rapidly than before, he began to make his way back toward his mother's bathroom window, the window with the screen out, the only one he could even hope to reach in time.

But he didn't make it. He was still about a dozen feet away when everything began to gray out.

CHAPTER EIGHTEEN

"Yeah? What'll ya have, bud?"

"Huh?"

"You want somethin' to eat or are ya just gonna set there all day?"

"All day?".

"Is there a echo in here or somethin'. Tell ya what, when ya want somethin', just let me know."

Nate looked around him. No ledge. No hospital.

Instead, he was sitting in a booth in some cafe. With red and gray alternating tiles on the floor, dingy and ragged gingham curtains in the windows, and food stains on the walls.

Again! It had happened again. He had blacked out and come to in a different place. And it suited him just fine this time.

But how? How was it happening? And what was causing it? It seemed just another puzzle to solve. He had more than his share of mysteries on his hands.

The waitress was approaching his table once more. She was tall, almost six feet, but she was also grossly overweight — by at least forty or fifty pounds. She looked more like she should be playing in the NFL than waiting tables.

"Decided on anything yet?"

Nate glanced down at the unopened menu before him, then back up at the waitress. "Uh, ah, just about.

Say, what time is it, anyway?"

She gave him an ugly stare, but she examined her watch briefly. "Nearly 10:30. And, yeah, you kin still git breakfus, if that's what you want."

"Oh...good! Thanks."

He waited for her to leave again, but this time she simply stood with her pad in her left hand and pencil poised ready to write with the other.

"Yeah, gimme a cup of coffee and some donuts. Got any donuts?"

"All gone. Still got some Danish, though. Want some a that?"

"What kind — oh, never mind, just bring any kind."

"Anythang else?"

"No. No, that'll be all."

She began to pivot her huge body around to leave, and Nate thought of something else he wanted.

"Yeah, there is one other thing."

She turned back, glaring at him.

"Uh, what *day* is this?"

She continued to stare, without speaking.

"I mean: Is it still Sunday?"

"Where you been, buddy? You think all these people would be in *here* on a Sunday. Hell, no. It's Monday!" With that, she swung back around and marched away before he had time to come up with any more questions.

Monday. Another day lost. But where had it gone?

The food came, and he downed it quickly, for he had remembered his last conversation with his mother. As he reached the cash register on wobbly legs, he also remembered the last time he'd gone into a restaurant after a blackout, and he hurriedly shoved a hand into his pants pocket. He found that he still had over half the money he'd taken from Casta's hiding place, so he paid for the food and stumbled out onto the street.

Trying to get his bearings, he stood for a moment,

looking all around, but this time he had no question as to his whereabouts. He spotted St. Thaddeus right down the street.

Mama? Maybe he should stop by to see her again before he took off to try and find Gamov. No, he couldn't do that. Lacy or some of his cohorts were probably still hanging around the hospital — or, at least, watching it.

He thought of hailing a cab, but, spotting a bus headed for campus, he boarded it instead. After all, he needed to hang on to as much of this cash as he could because he didn't know when he could get his hands on any more. He climbed off at the stop nearest the student union and walked quickly toward that neoclassical structure. Just inside, he found a "campus phone" with a campus directory and thumbed through it.

...Galvan...Galvez...Gamble...

"Aha!" he said aloud. "Gamov, Curtis R., M.D., Ph.D., Professor of Biochemistry and Assistant Director of Medical Research." That had to be him. It sounded too right not to be. His office was in Newton Hall, just a short walk away. And it was Monday, now, the sloppy waitress had said, so maybe he could find him in.

Just outside, he felt a finger tap him on the shoulder, and he almost swallowed his adam's apple. So close. Was he about to solve this and now they had found him?

Slowly, he swung around, ready to pounce on Lacy or whoever it might be.

"Nate! I thought that was you."

It was...

"Sandy. I'm Sandy, remember? You're not going to tell me you forgot me already, are you?"

"No. No, of course not." It was just good to see a friendly face.

"Oh, I closed the apartment door when I left. I tried to find a key lying around someplace, but I couldn't. I hope that's alright."

"Sure..."

"You left in such a hurry yesterday, I didn't know what to do."

"Oh, about that," he began, placing his right hand on one of her arms. "I'm really sorry. I didn't mean to leave you hangin' like that. It's just that — "

"I figured it had something to do with whatever was bothering you."

"Right! Yes, it did." He withdrew his hand, letting it dangle idly by his side.

"Don't worry. I've seen people do all kindsa funny things in my time. Did you get it taken care of?"

"Pardon?"

"Whatever it was that was bothering you."

"Uh, yeah... Well, no, not completely, but it's partly taken care of." His left leg had begun to twitch. He really ought to be on his way.

"That's good."

"Say, uh, Sandy, I, uh, got to run. I'll see you — "

"Where you headed?"

"To, uh, Newton."

"Got some kinda science class, huh?"

"Science...? Oh, yeah, sure."

"Well, I'm heading in that direction, too. You don't mind if I keep you company, do you?"

"Mind? No, why should I mind?"

They began to stroll southwest, toward the science complex.

"I don't think I've told you: I'm a senior business major."

"Oh, that's nice." He really didn't have time for this small talk. He needed to think.

"What's your major?"

"Major? Oh, I'm studying sociology."

"Oh, yeah. I took a sociology course once. I think it

was during my freshman year. How far along are you?"

"Huh." He could barely make out the uppermost story of Newton over Clemens Hall.

"Your rank...like freshman, sophomore ...?"

"Oh, that. Senior. I'll be graduating next month."

"You, too? That's nice. Look, if I'm bothering you, I can get lost."

He wished she would. "No, no. You don't need to do that." Why couldn't he say what he was thinking? But this girl had found him once and returned him safely to his apartment. He didn't want to be unnecessarily rude.

What was he going to ask Gamov, anyway? What could the man tell him to help solve this mystery? What did the Dinosaur Project have to do with the attempts on his life? Then, it occurred to him: nothing, maybe. Perhaps there was no relationship between what Kidder had heard about "Dinah's kids" and the "Dinosaur Project." Probably he was just grasping at straws. He thought about veering off and heading back toward his apartment. No, it wouldn't hurt to check this thing out. After all, it was the only straw he had to grasp at. So what if it turned out to be a dead-end venture? He couldn't be any worse off then he was before.

"Look over there!" Sandy shouted, pointing toward Newton, which had just become fully visible as they came around Clemens.

A crowd was gathering in front of the building, but Nate could see a flashing red light above their heads.

"What's happenin', bro?" Nate asked another young black whom he'd had classes with and who was standing near the rear of the crowd.

"Somebody's hurt. Don't know nothin' else."

Then Nate spotted Martin Yeager making his way through the crowd. He rushed toward the familiar face.

"What is it, Martin?"

"Nate, where you been? We been worried sick about

you. When you didn't show up for Cassie's funeral, Babes and I went lookin' — "

"I'm fine, Martin. But tell me what's goin' on here?"

"An explosion of some kinds in one of the labs. Somebody got hurt. I think it was one of the professors. Don't know who."

Could it be? No, he had to get his imagination under control. "You see him?"

"No, but I heard *it*. I was in another part of the building at the time."

"Yeah? And you don't know who...?"

"Some old guy, somebody told me. Been teaching here for years."

"Oh?" Come on, Nate. There must be hundreds of teachers who had been here for years.

"Sorry, that's all I know. Got to get on to my next class."

Martin started to step away from Nate, but Nate grabbed him by the arm. "How bad's he hurt?"

The other shrugged. "Sorry ..."

Nate released his grip, nodding.

"Gotta run. Glad to see you around again. I'll pass the word on to the others that you're okay," Yeager added, stepping away.

"Yeah, do that," Nate called after him.

He glanced around and saw that Sandy was staring at his face.

"What's — " she began, but he waved a hand in front of her, signaling silence, for he could hear a voice addressing the crowd.

"...step back, please."

Those in front of him began to move backwards, and a foot came down hard on his. A stocky, blonde guy looked around.

"Sorry," he offered. But Nate paid little attention to him, sidestepping the further backward movements of the crowd. He felt a hand in his, and realized it must be Sandy's.

"I gotta get up there," he said, turning to face her.

She nodded as he began to lead her, bucking the movement of the crowd, pushing forward. They were nearly trampled several more times before they made it to the front of the pack of on-lookers.

A fire truck and a police car were off slightly to his right, with an ambulance almost immediately in front of them. He saw a man with a megaphone standing on the steps of the building, but he was looking toward the structure's front door, not toward the crowd. Nate thought about going up to the man and asking what he wanted to know, but he decided against it, for he had just begun to pick up snatches of conversation. He looked all around in every direction, though he was still unable to locate its source.

"...right. Better call 'em in. Looks a little suspicious to me, too."

"Okay, have it sealed off."

Arson! They were talking about arson. Two fireman were talking about — but wait! There weren't any firemen standing near him. Oh, shit! Surely it wasn't starting again. Not the voices.

He grasped Sandy's hand more firmly and was just about to start up the steps to make his inquiry when the man swung around to face the crowd, placing the megaphone to his mouth.

"Stand back, please. Please, move back."

Behind the man, through the glass front door of Newton Hall, Nate could see others approaching, and they were carrying something. As they reached the door, he recognized it as a stretcher. Through the door they moved and down the steps. As they came near the ambulance, someone stepped up and opened the doors for them. But Nate knew they were in no rush, for the person they carried on the stretcher was completely covered by a sheet. Nevertheless, a few seconds later, both men climbed inside the ambulance, and the vehicle sped away.

Nate continued to hold Sandy's hand and stand and watch the front door for several more minutes. Gradually, the crowd began to thin out, and, at last, he made his way toward the man with the megaphone who was now coming down from the steps.

"Who was that?" he asked the man, pointing in the direction the ambulance had taken.

The other looked him squarely in the eyes. "It was a teacher, Professor Gamov."

And suddenly Nate knew that he hadn't been "grasping at straws," at all — that, indeed, "Dinah's kids" and the "Dinosaur Project" referred to the same thing. That whatever it was, whatever it meant, it had something to do with the reason people had been trying to kill him. Also, he knew that, more than ever, he had to find out about that project.

Without thinking about it, he squeezed Sandy's hand even more firmly and pulled her toward the entrance of the building. As he did so, however, he felt a hand on his arm. Glancing around, he saw that it was the man with the megaphone.

"We're asking that nobody enter the building right now. If you have classes in Newton, they've been cancelled for the time being."

Nate hardly heard the words, for he wasn't concerned with trivial matters like classes at this moment. He jerked his arm loose and proceeded up the steps.

"Hey, wait!" the man shouted, running after him and leaping in his path. But Nate shoved him aside and reached for the door.

"Kid! Didn't you hear me? I said you couldn't go in there."

It wasn't the man's warning which stopped him, but something entirely different. Just as he swung the door wide, his head came alive again with the strange thoughts...

Piss! That's him right there!

And he knew the "him" referred to Nathan Tibbetts.

Swinging around, he jerked Sandy along as together they ran down the steps and plunged among the last few stragglers who had formed the crowd.

CHAPTER NINETEEN

Sandy pulled back on him. "What's wrong?" she shouted over the roar of a dozen conversations taking place all around them.

"I can't tell you who, but *somebody's* after me."

"But I thought — "

"I've got to find a place to hide. I'm sorry if I've involved you," he told her, abruptly releasing her hand.

"Involved me in what?"

"I don't know, but I've got to go."

He turned away and had taken almost a half dozen steps at a near-run when he heard her scream over the din.

"Wait!"

He glanced around, slowing up slightly, and he saw her running toward him, her full skirt flapping up high above her knees. A few seconds later, she overtook him, grabbing him by the left arm with both her hands.

"My car. Let's get to my car. It's parked in H17 — between here and the union."

He nodded. If she wanted to help, he certainly wasn't going to refuse. He could use every bit he could get now. Waving with his right hand, he signaled for her to take the lead, adding, "I don't know which way."

She dropped her left hand off his, tugging him along with the right. "Then, come on."

A second later, they were both charging across the

campus at breakneck speed. Several times, they had to dodge groups of on-coming students and leap over obstructions like bushes and markers, but Sandy showed no inclination to slow up until they reached the lot.

"Now, where did I park the damn thing?" she asked, looking around frantically at the edge of the lot. Then: "There!" Pointing toward an ancient VW Karmann Ghia.

Less than a minute later, she was unlocking the car and they were scurrying inside.

"See anybody following us?" she asked.

Nate looked back in the direction they had come. "No, but — "

"Good. Even if they are, we should be able to lose 'em."

He heard the engine roar, and the car lurched backwards, out of the parking place, then forward, throwing a pile of gravel up in its wake.

"My place, okay?" she asked, as she charged out of the lot. "If somebody's after you, yours might not be too safe."

Good thinking! Maybe stumbling into this girl was his lucky bonanza.

"Sure!" he said. And a good thing, too, for she'd already turned in the opposite direction from his apartment.

The next five minutes saw them slide around a half-dozen corners, narrowly miss a jaywalker and his dog, run two stop signs, and swing left against a red light.

"You always drive like this?" he inquired, at last.

She grinned slightly and glanced over at him. "No, not always — only when I'm trying to lose a tail. That alright?"

"It has to be. You're behind the wheel."

Her smile disappeared. "Well, it's for — "

"Me! I know that. You're doing it for me. I just hope

we get to your place in one piece."

The Karmann Ghia screeched to a halt.

"We're here!"

"Good!"

"I don't think anybody was behind us, anyway, but I didn't want to take any chances." She slapped him on the left knee. "Let's go!"

She jumped out before he could even start to get up from his bucket seat.

Following her across the street, he noticed that she didn't even seem to be winded. He pushed himself to catch up with her.

"How'd you do it?" he asked.

"What, lose 'em? Keep the car on the road? What?"

"No. All that running."

"Oh, that.... I ran track until last year. Got boring. I'd done it since high school. My interests just drifted elsewhere, I guess. I still do a little jogging, though."

Her apartment was also a second-story affair, but it was a good deal different from the one he'd shared with Casta. Nate found Sandy's apartment modern, with practically new furnishings.

After she'd seated Nate, Sandy scurried into the toilet. When she returned to the living room moments later, she had discarded her blouse and skirt and was dressed in only a bra and panty set.

Nate caught his breath as she slipped down beside him on the gleaming leatherette sofa.

"Oh, I'm sorry. Does this bother you?" she asked, touching her bra with her right hand. "I always run around here like this, and, after Saturday night and yesterday, I didn't suppose..."

"It's just that you have such a terrific body, you could drive a man nuts," he said.

"That's the general idea — most of the time. Isn't it?"

Nate tried to smile, but he couldn't take his mind off

what had just occurred.

Sandy picked up the implication of his expression. "I'm still ready to listen any time you want me to."

Why not? She'd just saved him, maybe for the second time.

"Some really weird things have been happening to me in the last week or so," he began. "I was climbing a rock cliff with some friends and the rope broke, then two guys try to knife me in an alley, then my girlfriend — really, she was my fiance — gets killed — "

"Oh, I didn't know. Maybe that explains — "

"Explains why I've been running around like a zombie?"

"I didn't say that."

"You didn't have to. But that's not it. There are some people out to *kill* me."

She placed a warm hand on his thigh and looked him squarely in the eyes. "You sure these things aren't merely horrible coincidences?"

"Damn right, I'm sure. Cause that ain't all. You see, the other night — I don't remember which — two dudes kidnap me from a friend's house, handcuff me, blindfold me, gag me, and take me some other place and lock me up."

She jerked her hand away and covered her mouth which had dropped open. "Goddamn!... Who were they?"

"I didn't see them. Not really. But then, I did 'see' them, if you understand what I... No, doesn't make any sense. Forget it."

"No, tell me about it."

"I can't."

"Why not?"

"Because if I did, you'd think I was some kind of loony, that's why not."

"Nate, trust me, I — "

"I said, 'No.' I can't. Not yet."

"Why?"

"'Why?' Just because I can't, that's why. Because I don't really understand it, myself."

"Why don't you tell me, and I'll help you understand it. We can try to understand it together. You've got to trust somebody someday. You've got to stop running and try to understand it."

"'Stop running' How do you know I've been running?"

"Well, I think that's pretty obvious. Besides, what do you think we just did? We just ran away from somebody. Who? Who was it back there that made you run away?"

"I told you I don't know. Why don't you believe me?"

"Alright, alright." She held up her left hand, fingers together. "I just thought you might be able to figure it out, that's all."

"Don't you think I've been trying?"

"What was all that about back at Newton?"

"I was looking for someone. I needed to talk with someone."

"Who? Dr. Gamov?"

Now he stared wide-eyed, his brow wrinkled. "How did you know that?"

"It didn't take a super detective. One look at your face when that fellow told you who the dead man on the stretcher was said it all."

"Yeah?"

"Well, not all, maybe, but some of it. What did Gamov have to do with you?"

He shifted around on the sofa, which suddenly seemed like a most uncomfortable place to sit. "Not me," he said, finally. "My mother. He had something to do with my mother."

"What?"

"I'm not sure."

"Tell me." Her eyes, staring into his, seemed almost to

have hypnotic powers, compelling him to speak.

"My mother — actually, my mother and my father, but he'd been dead for years — were involved in a project run by Gamov before I was born."

"What's that got to do with you?"

"I told you: I don't — "

"Yes, I know you told me, but you must have had some reason for believing — "

"Okay, here's what it is, but don't ask me what it means: My friend — the one whose house I was kidnapped from, remember?" She nodded.

"Well, he told me he overheard the dudes who captured me call me 'Dinah's kid' — the 'last of Dinah's kids.' Only my Mama's name ain't Dinah, it's Sara. Anyway, I remembered something about this project, or rather something she'd said, which turned out to be about the project."

Sandy brought both hands up in front of her, cupped in half-circles. "Then, what is it?"

"They called Gamov's project the 'Dinosaur Project'."

"Which means...?"

"How should I know what it means? I told you it didn't make any sense, didn't I?"

She shrugged. "Maybe it's code."

"Sure, I guess that's what it is, but what does it mean: 'Dinosaur Project.' They were studying cancer — trying to develop a cure — not fossils. What do dinosaurs have to do with cancer, anyway?"

"I guess you'll just have to figure that out."

"Sure, that's easy for you to say. Nobody's running around trying to kill you."

She glanced away, but not before Nate caught sight of the glistening in her eyes.

Neither said anything for more than a minute.

Finally, he reached over and placed a hand on her shoulder. "I'm sorry."

Sandy looked back around at him, trying to smile through her tears. "It's alright, Nate. I was only trying to help you solve your problem. Maybe I pushed too hard."

And she leaned over and kissed him on the lips. Her warm, throbbing body pressed against him was more than he could take. His hand went around behind her and he began to massage her buttocks through her panties. Soon, he was stretched out on the sofa, and she was lying atop him. Her lips rotated around and around on his with passionate tenderness. Her whole body quivered as he felt himself become more and more aroused. Suddenly, she stopped and jumped up, jerking her remaining clothes off and tossing them to the floor. Then she helped him out of his before she mounted him again, and this time it was for real.

Afterwards, they lay intertwined, their lips pressed together but unmoving.

Sandy broke the silence.

"I know this thing is awful, but let me help you, Nate. You remember what I told you yesterday? Well, I mean it. Maybe I've only known you a couple of days, but already you really mean something to me. You're not just — well, not just a good fuck. Let me be your woman. Together we can lick this. We'll figure it out — together."

His woman? *His* woman? No, that wasn't possible. His woman was dead, and he had caused it. He didn't know how or why, but it had been his fault.

He pulled away from Sandy, stood up, and walked into her modern, gleaming bathroom. Christ, seeing all this shining porcelain was enough to make a fellow sick. He relieved himself and cleaned himself up, then walked back into the living room, where he found that she was still lying the way he had left her.

Avoiding her piercing eyes, he slipped back into his clothes.

"What now?" she asked, at last.

But still he avoided looking at her.

Yeah, what now?

"You hungry?" She seemed to be trying a different approach. He couldn't go on ignoring her forever.

"A little, I guess."

"What would you like?"

He let his eyes make contact with hers again. But they were just ordinary blue eyes, devoid of any magical qualities. "Are you going to start that again?"

"Oh, yeah, I see what you mean. You're talking about our discussion over breakfast yesterday."

He nodded, trying to smile.

"What say I just fix us something, and if you don't like it, you can lump it?"

"Now that's more reasonable. That's what Mama always did?"

"What about Casta?"

"Oh, she fixed whatever she wanted, too, but most of the time we worked together on the meals." Then, it hit him — he didn't remember giving Casta's name. Oh, what the hell, he'd probably said it a hundred times when she picked him up Sunday night, and Sandy had just put two-and-two together, as she appeared adept at doing.

"Then maybe you'd like to help me in the kitchen, too."

"Uh, yeah, sure. Why not?"

At least, it would give him something to do.

She fixed hamburgers and made a salad. He peeled and fried the potatoes and heated a can of beans. A good old American staple.

As they were eating, she shifted the conversation back around to the heavy stuff.

"Nate, I want you to stay with me tonight. I want you to stay *until* we're sure you're safe."

He held up a hand. "I couldn't — "

"You think I want your death on my conscience? Hell, no! You're staying put till this thing is settled. What if I let you go out there and some nut shoots you down?"

"Okay, if you're sure."

"Sure, I'm sure. Now, shut up and finish eating." But she was grinning again.

They lay together in her queen-sized waterbed sloshing around and watching TV afterwards. But he couldn't concentrate on the programming. His mind was running over and over everything he knew or could remember about the last few days — which wasn't very much. Not very much that seemed helpful in his quest for answers, anyway. He thought about telling Sandy about the headaches, the blackouts, and the voices, but he didn't want to chance losing her confidence at this point.

They ate another meal in early evening, then returned to bed.

Around 10:30, she turned the boob tube off and lay snuggled up next to him, rubbing his chest. He knew she was trying to arouse him again, but he simply couldn't get into the mood. Finally, after 11, he told her so, and she turned out the lights.

But sleep didn't come easy. He tossed and turned long after he heard her snoring. Finally, he got up and went to the toilet again. That didn't seem to help much, however. Sometime after 1, he, at last, began to doze off.

The clock-radio jerked him out of a deep sleep, and he bolted upright in the bed.

"Oh, damn," Sandy mumbled. "Why did I have to get stuck with an 8 o'clock class?" She puffed up her pillow. "I'm not going, that's all there is to it."

About fifteen minutes later, she did struggle up and into the shower. When she'd finished bathing, Nate assured her that he felt perfectly safe in her apartment and that she should go on to class.

"If I didn't have a big test coming up..."

"Go! I'll be fine."

They fixed bowls of dry cereal and sat across from each other, munching it.

"Maybe I really ought to go to classes, too," he said, thinking aloud. "It's been a hell of a long time. How am I ever going to graduate next month if I don't catch up?"

"Are you *nuts*? You're really nuts, you know? There's some goddamn murderer out there" — she waved a hand toward the window — "after you, and you talk about going to fuckin' classes."

"But I haven't been in God knows how long." Nate certainly didn't know how long it had been.

"Who cares? Listen, I'm not going myself if that kind of thing is going to worry you."

He held up both hands. "It doesn't. I was just thinking, that's all. I wasn't really planning to go."

She squinted at him. "You sure? 'Cause I really don't have to go. Screw the damn test."

"No, you go on — please. I need some time to think, anyway."

She offered a not-too-convincing smile and shrugged.

About ten minutes later — after she had received assurances from him again that he would stay put — she left, a stack of books in her arms.

But, despite what he had told Sandy, he found that, as the day wore on, he was simply piddling around the apartment. He even tried to watch television again. Everything but confront his problem. Finally, around mid-afternoon, he found he couldn't run away from it any longer. He knew he had to have answers. And the more he thought about it, the fewer the alternatives he could find available to him.

He didn't like the decision he finally reached. But he saw no avoiding it. The only way he knew of getting the answers he needed was to pick up the trail where he'd last left off. He had to get into Gamov's lab — and he had to do it *tonight*.

INTERLUDE J

"He seems to have gone after your bait, Cougar."

"Good. Do you think he smells a trap?"

"No, not at this point."

"Excellent. Things seem, at last, to be coming together at your end, Panther."

"I believe they are, sir."

"And you are to be commended for your farsightedness in removing Gamov and that file before he could get to it. Undoubtedly, he would've been able to put it all together if he'd either read the information in that folder or talked to the good doctor."

"I believe so, sir."

"All right, Panther, this has to be the last attempt, whether or not you've gotten the information you need to do it safely. Further, we can no longer be concerned with making it look accidental. The danger is paramount. For the well-being of the country, we must act immediately. So, get the word out to scrap all other procedures and use only the most direct methods. Just get him now!"

CHAPTER TWENTY

"You're what?" The disgust was evident on her face. "Now, that's *just great.*"

"You have a better suggestion?" he asked.

She looked away from him. "Surely, there's 'some other way," she said, finally.

"Name it!"

Her penetrating eyes found his again. "Nate, what are you trying to prove — really?"

"Nothing! I simply have to know what happened in those experiments — why somebody is trying to kill me because of them."

"But why can't it wait?" Her eyes seemed to be pleading with him.

"You can see that, surely. Every minute I wait, the greater the likelihood that whoever is trying to get me will be successful. For the first time, I think I'm onto something that might be meaningful — that might give me the answers I need. I just thought, since you've done so much for me, I should tell you what I'm going to do."

"Get yourself arrested for breaking and entering, that's what." Her look of disgust was back.

"The police are the least of my worries — except for how they fit into this. And I won't know that until I find out what this means, will I?"

"Then, I'm going with you. I can't have you going off like this alone, can I?"

"*Yes!*" he shouted. "I *am* going alone. I'm not going to let you put your life in danger, too."

"Nate — "

He held up a hand. "*No!*"

Grabbing her aggressively by both arms, he pulled her to him and planted a kiss firmly on her lips.

"See ya," he said, opening her apartment door.

"Dammit, Nathan Tibbetts, you come back here."

He closed the door and ran down the steps, ignoring the elevator which was stopping on the second floor.

Just as he hit the sidewalk, he heard a rattling and banging sound in the direction of the apartment, then —

"Hey!"

Looking around, he saw Sandy sticking her head out of her apartment window.

"Here, at least, take the car," she shouted, tossing something toward him.

A few feet away, he saw a set of keys fall onto the sidewalk.

"Okay, I'll do *that*," he shouted back, scooping up the keys and dashing across the street to her Karmann Ghia.

He'd never driven one of these little cars before, but he found it handling perfectly as he sped away.

Would he find what he needed in Gamov's lab? Would he learn anything valuable about those experiments over two decades ago? Obviously, someone had been afraid of what he might learn, so the professor had paid with his life. Nate tried to come up with possibilities for what he might find, but he drew a blank. Then, he found something else which he had to focus on.

In his rearview mirror, he'd seen them, a pair of headlights that stayed doggedly behind him. Around every curve, during every lane change, following every turn. It was a "tail." No question about it.

Following through on instinct, he slammed the car's accelerator downward, and the Karmann Ghia shot forward, as he'd seen it move during the previous day with a female driver behind the wheel. He found he couldn't make the turns as sharply or zip in and out of lanes quite as fast as Sandy had. After all, it was her car, and she'd had plenty of practice time. But it performed for him. Though not quite well enough. Every time he looked in the mirror, the other vehicle was still there.

Nate found himself nudging just a little more out of the VW. But still he had company.

Something had to work. It always did in the movies. Somehow, they always shook off the tails. But that was the movies, and this was real life. Nevertheless, there had to be a way.

He found his path suddenly blocked. All lanes full of traffic, and nobody trying to pass anybody else. The lights behind him were closing. He had to try something.

Gritting his teeth, he swerved to the left — into a lane for oncoming traffic — and pushed the accelerator all the way down.

Around a truck.

Another sports car.

And...

The sound of horns.

Something was heading directly toward him! Swerving sharply right, he squeezed between the other sports car — which had speeded up, attempting to block him — and a large sedan. There couldn't have been more than a dozen feet's clearance in front *and* back, total.

He released a lung full of air.

But he found himself locked in between the two vehicles.

He tried slowing, to drop back from the lead car, but the other slowed, too. The sports model behind continued to tailgate. Finally, he saw an opening and zipped into the right lane, and soon he was clipping along again.

However, he realized that his tail was back.

What now?

Onto a side street.

The tail hung on tightly.

A left turn. He still had a tail.

A right turn, another left, followed by another quick right.

But he couldn't lose the tail.

More speed. The tail matched his speed.

Down an alley. Turn. Speed up. Over a hill, and out of sight of the tail for a moment. Into a crowded parking lot. And he watched the tail sail on by. It was a cab.

His breathing became more normal, and finally he felt enough in control to start the car again and move out. He found he'd gone a long way out of his way, but he didn't want any company now. He would be taking enough chances, as it was.

About three blocks from Newton, he parked Sandy's car and continued on foot. Anything to buy a little time. He didn't want to leave it too close to his destination. Maybe he wouldn't need it for a quick getaway. It was a gamble any way he looked at it.

When he arrived at Newton, he found it looking quite normal. There were no police cars cruising by or a guard standing duty at the door. Perhaps whatever investigation was being done had already been completed. He strolled inside along with several other students, those with the evident misfortune to have night classes, and no one tried to bar him this time. He also heard no "voices" talking about him. In fact, *everything* seemed normal — *too normal.*

"Hey, bro, what's hap'nin'?"

Nate felt himself jump as he whirled around. It was the student he'd asked the same question yesterday outside Newton.

"Not much, my man. What about you?" He was trying to be cool, but was he *over*doing it?

The other raised a hand and swiveled it back and forth. "So-so. Could be better. Listen here, you got a class in here tonight, too?"

"Uh...well, not exactly. I'm, uh, supposed to meet somebody here."

"Oh, I get you — your woman." The other jabbed him lightly in the stomach and winked.

Nate shrugged and offered a half-hearted smile.

"Is it that fox you was with yesterday?"

"Uh, yeah, uh..."

"Umh-umh. She's one nice-looking piece of ass." The other held up a free hand. "Hope I didn't offend you or nothin'. But she is mighty fine lookin'."

"You know her?"

"No. You not fixin' to ditch her, are you? Cause if you are, I wouldn't mind it if you tossed her my way."

He had to cut this and get on with business, if —

But the other beat him to it. "Gotta run, my man. See you around."

"Yeah, see ya."

Whew. He was glad all that small-talk crap was over. He hoped he didn't run into anybody else he knew.

Gamov's office and lab were in the basement of Newton, he discovered, checking the directory in the front lobby, so he headed directly there.

However, at the bottom of the steps, he found a rope and a printed sign stating that the lower level was off limits pending the outcome of a fire investigation.

Oh, well, he wasn't going to let a little rope and sign stop him.

Stepping over the rope, he found himself in a darkened hallway, with only exit signs to offer light. Not knowing in which direction Gamov's office was located, he moved down the hall to the right a short distance, then stopped and closed his eyes. It was an old trick he'd learned as a boy. With the increase in darkness, his eyes more quickly adjusted. Opening them a moment later, he found that it had worked as usual. He was beginning to distinguish objects again.

Slowly, he moved off once more, examining each door he came to, looking for either 42 (lab) or 44 (office) or the name "Curtis Gamov." All the way down the right-hand side. Nothing. Back up the left. Still nothing, He moved past the stairway, and the first door he came to not only read "44," but had Gamov's name and title below, as well. However, there was another of the fire inspection notices pasted there, also.

Nate turned the knob. Of course, it was locked, but he'd learned long ago not to overlook the obvious. Sometimes people went off and accidentally left doors unlocked, and there was no need trying to pick a lock that wasn't locked.

Reaching into his pocket, he removed a small pick he had put together at Sandy's house, and he set to work trying to get the lock to release. He'd never done this much, but he knew how.

"Legs" Barlow had shown both Kidder and him how one time, and the three of them had sneaked into "Old Man" Thompson's garage. They hadn't found anything of value, and the two of them were anxious to leave but Legs had insisted they take something just on principle. "Can't go busting in without gittin' somethin'," he had said. "Wudn't look right." So Nate had chosen an old crescent wrench.

Nearly five minutes passed, and Nate found that the lock was stubbornly remaining locked. Legs had made it seem so easy, but this was probably a much more complicated lock. Still, the principles of lock-picking should remain constant.

He found that his palms had become sweaty, and he wiped first one, then the other on his jean legs.

Maybe he needed more light. Perhaps then, he could see what to do. No, you don't need much light to pick a lock, just a good sense of touch and hearing.

A dryness in his throat made him wish he had a mouthful of water. Or a Pepsi. Or even a beer. He didn't like beer much, but it would do in a pinch, and this was a pinch. His throat was parched and dry. Desert dry.

Then, finally, the lock clicked, and a second later, Nate eased the door open. And what he saw across the room made him curse himself for his ill-preparedness. It was a window. Even though this was a basement office, the building evidently wasn't completely underground on this side, and there was a window near the top of the room. Nate knew he needed a flashlight, for if anyone spotted a light on down here, the cops might swarm in on him before he had a chance to get away. He thought about leaving long enough to obtain a flashlight, then coming back, but he discarded that idea. He was just too close to turn back now. Answers might be awaiting him inside one of the two filing cabinets he could dimly make out. So he flipped on the light and rushed toward them.

Pulling open the top drawer of the first one, he found something instantly to be thankful for. They seemed well-organized, with files all in alphabetical order. That seemed reasonable. Since Gamov had been a scientist, he probably had an orderly mind. But such rational thinking didn't always prevail with this kind, Nate knew.

Quickly through the files, his eyes scanned. The top drawer ended with "Calcium," so Nate shoved it closed and jerked open the second drawer, proceeding through the "D's." Nothing. No "Dinosaur Project," nor anything on "Dinah." Slowly, he pushed the file drawer shut, disappointment pervading his system. Intellectually, he knew he hadn't really been expecting to find anything helpful, but his emotions had led him down the primrose path of hope.

His eyes alighted on the second cabinet, and suddenly he felt hope renewed within him. Perhaps they were for two different sets of files.

They were! The top drawer of the second cabinet began with "Acceptor." Nate felt a smile creep across his face as he jerked it open. Finding that the drawer stopped short of his goal at "Digitalis," he quickly turned to the second, searching through it even before the top one had closed completely. Here, however, his disappointment was renewed, for its files began with "Dinoflagellida" and jumped to "Diphtheria." Disgusted and disappointed, Nate slammed the drawer. Then, as an afterthought he checked, without much expectation, in the next one for "Project." Still nothing.

But, as he was closing the third drawer, his eyes caught the Label on the second, which he had just examined: "DiNA-Hematome," it read. Hurriedly, he yanked the drawer open again to double check. No, the first file was definitely "Dinoflagellida." But it had slid down slightly, the way files do when one has been removed from in front and the space not redistributed. It was obvious: *A file folder was missing!*

He closed the cabinet and read it again. Not "Dinah," as he had been spelling it in his mind, but "DiNA." Why, it wasn't a secret code, at all. It was more a convenience term which someone must have nicknamed "Dinosaur." Plainly, Gamov had been involved in genetic experiments, in efforts to change the gene structure. But what went wrong? Why did the experiments stop?

Why weren't they publicized? But that, too, became obvious to Nate. Gamov must have perceived them as a failure. And perhaps they were. Wasn't Mama, at this very moment, dying of cancer? But someone saw some value in Gamov's research, and whoever that someone was, he had beaten Nate to the file folder that contained the information on Gamov's DNA experiments and killed Gamov in the process.

Nate swallowed hard, and tried to salivate and clear the dryness out of his mouth. He was too late. Again!

But how did it involve him? Why were "they" trying to kill him because of some experiments conducted before he was born, before...?

Suddenly, he became aware of "it." He had always heard stories about people being able to "feel" others staring at them, but he had never believed in such — until now. And *now* he had no doubt about it. Someone was out there watching him, studying his every move.

The desert sand in his mouth suddenly felt as though it was being baked by the scorching rays of an equatorial sun. He tried to swallow again, but nothing would go down.

Should he swing around and try to catch whoever it was off guard? No, not yet. Don't let him know that he had been spotted.

Think! He had to think. How was he going to get out of this one...?

Abruptly, he became aware that it wasn't a "he" watching him. No, the pair of eyes fixed on him had the "feel" of femininity. Nate closed his own eyes and let his mind dwell on that thought. Gradually, the face to go with those eyes became clearer and clearer. At last, no more concentration was necessary.

Without budging or even offering to turn around, he spoke, addressing the woman with the penetrating eyes.

"Come in, Sandy," he said, simply.

CHAPTER TWENTY-ONE

Behind him, he could now hear the sound of footfalls, but still he didn't turn.

"How long have you known I was here?" she asked.

"Long enough."

At last he turned and faced her, half expecting to see a gun pointed at his chest.

But she held no weapons.

"You were the one in the cab, weren't you?" he asked.

She nodded. "Yes."

"I should have caught on to you earlier, I guess, but I had too many other things on my mind."

"But, Nate — "

"You can save all that. Just give me the answers I want."

"Nate, I'm trying to tell you — "

"Goddammit, woman, I want some fucking damn answers now," he shouted. "*Now!* Do you hear?"

"I'm trying to tell you that I don't have *any* answers!" she shouted back.

He took a step toward her, his fists clenched, fire burning in his eyes.

"Nate, honest," she pleaded. "I don't know *anything!*"

He paused less than two feet from her. "Then why did you follow me here?"

"I was frightened for you. Since you wouldn't let me come along, I took maters into my own hands."

He stared into those eyes and tried to read truth.

"Nate, please believe me." She grabbed his right fist and drew it to her lips, kissing it repeatedly. "I...I think — no, I *know*, I love you."

Angrily, he jerked the fist away. "Shit, woman. You don't know what love is. It's more than just humpin'."

There was fire in his eyes, and he saw an image of Casta lying dead under that awning. Gritting his teeth, he opened the fist which she had just kissed and shoved her away from him. She went sprawling on the floor several feet away.

Tears glimmered in her eyes. "No, Nate, please. I really, *really* don't know a damn thing. I simply couldn't let you come here alone. That's all."

There was a sudden clatter in the hallway, and Nate shifted his focus in that direction.

"He's *not* alone," he heard someone say only seconds before two men stepped into view. One he recognized immediately as the man who had come to his apartment and identified himself as Sergeant Lacy.

Both his fists relaxed at his side as Nate caught sight of the pistols which each of them held. He could feel the moisture trickling down his temples.

"*We've* come to keep you company," Lacy added.

Still, Nate offered no response.

The two men with the guns halted about ten feet away.

"You've been quite a slippery fish to catch," Lacy continued, showing pearly white teeth in a sly grin. "But you're hooked now. This is the end of the line."

Lacy's focus shifted to Sandy, and he waved the gun around a bit. "And I'm afraid it's goodbye to you, too, sweetheart. You shouldn't a let yourself get mixed up with the likes of this one."

A surge of guilt ran through Nate's body as he saw Sandy still lying on the cold floor of Gamov's laboratory.

He turned and stared at Lacy, the fire in his eyes even more intense than before. "Why?" he demanded. "What has she done? What have *I* done?"

Lacy only grinned.

Nate felt droplets of sweat begin to drip off the tip of his chin as he stood "frozen," transfixed staring at the rows of malicious teeth in the other man's mouth. Then, suddenly, he felt his attention being drawn away from Lacy, and, no matter how hard he tried, he couldn't maintain his concentration on either the man or the weapon the other held, pointed directly at him. What he was feeling now had become very familiar during the last few days, but still he couldn't prevent himself from cringing as the bolt of pain creased his forehead. However, it was apparent immediately that this one was different from the other attacks, for there was no sensation of dizziness. Instead, Nate felt a flurry of images enter his mind, as he realized that whatever answer Lacy might have given to his last question would have been superfluous. For now he "knew" all the answers. He "knew" *everything!* The headaches, the blackouts, the attempts on his life, Gamov's project. They were all there spelled out in full detail inside his head, along with the true identity of his pursurer — *whose mind had just unwittingly supplied those answers.* Nate also knew that that same pursurer even now stood barely out of sight in the darkened hallway.

"Come in, 'Panther' — or should I say, Babes!" Nate shouted.

A second later, Babes Carmichael stepped into view.

"It's been a long hunt, Nate. You were a hard man to bring down," he said.

"I'm not *down* yet!"

"Now that's just a formality." Babes snapped his fingers and motioned toward the other two men. "Pop 'em, and let's get the hell out of here."

Lacy and the man standing beside him raised their guns and aimed them directly at Nate's head. But Nate did not flinch. The dryness was gone out of his throat and the sweatiness from his palms as he simply closed his eyes and concentrated.

Abruptly, Lacy and the other man both swung around, pointing their weapons at each other. Nate could "see" the gleam of terror in Lacy's eyes and that his gun hand trembled as he shoved the pistol against the other man's forehead even as his partner's gun pointed at him.

"No!" Nate heard the unnamed man scream an instant before he squeezed the trigger, simultaneously to the split-second that Lacy did the same.

The two crumpled to the floor, dead long before their bodies touched the hard tile surface.

Nate opened his eyes and stared at Babes.

"You waited just a little too long," he said to the other man. Out of corners of his eyes, he could see Sandy at last begin to rise, holding her stomach.

"We underestimated you, I guess. All the other DiNA kids were easy to eliminate."

"None of them were descended from *two* parents whose genes had been tampered with."

Babes' right cheek had begun to twitch. "Only it wasn't really tampering," he offered. "Dr. Gamov *really* was searching for a cure for cancer."

"And my people were his guinea pigs, as blacks have always been."

The other was now staring at the floor. "Well, look what he did. The stupid bastard! He unlocked a Pandora's box and created a Frankenstein's Monster at the same time."

Nate clenched his fists again and squinted at Carmichael. "The damn government's just paranoid, that's all — sending all you fuckin' CONTROL agents out to get us."

Babes returned his stare. "We weren't trying to *get you* or anybody else to begin with. When they realized what Gamov had done, we were just sent to observe. But then the changes began. In every one but you! They all had powers. Don't you see, we had to eliminate them? We couldn't have them running around destroying the country. It's been over a year since the last one was taken care of. The last one but you, of course. I was beginning to hope — I really hoped — that you were different. But no! You have it, too! Only *worse.*"

"Why did you people see us as such a threat? After all, scientists have made some outstanding discoveries by accident before. Why did you think this one was different?"

"Because mankind wasn't supposed to have the full use of his damn brain, that's why!" Carmichael practically spat out the words. "We didn't need it before, and we don't need it now. But that fool Gamov went to mixing and mingling the genetic code — messing around with things he had no business with — and not only changed such things as your completion and eye color but also unlocked areas of the mind that had been dormant since the beginning of time. Maybe someday mankind would have developed the full use of his brain, but *not now!* We're not ready for it yet!"

Hatred burned in Babes' eyes, but Nate did not try to avoid them, even when the other shoved an accusing finger toward him and added: "*And you're not ready yet either!*"

Slowly, Carmichael let his hand drop to his side.

"Well, I don't have much of a choice, do I?" Nate said, finally.

The two of them stood facing each other, jaws set, eyes locked in combat, but without spoken words, for what seemed like hours to Nate, but he realized must have been mere seconds.

At last, he broke the grip of Carmichael's eyes and glanced down at the two bodies less than a dozen feet in front of him. A puddle of blood surrounded Lacy's face, but it had already begun to congeal at the edges.

Without looking up again, Nate stepped slowly forward and over the body of the unidentified man — past Carmichael and through the doorway and into the hall.

Pausing, he looked back at Sandy.

"You coming?" he asked.

A few seconds later, she stood by his side, grasping his right hand firmly.

Together, they began to stroll slowly down the hall, toward the roped off stairs. Nate perceived the trembling in her body as it brushed against his, but he felt no need to rush, not even when he "saw" Babes withdraw a gun from the holster attached to the back of his belt. Nor did he attempt to turn around. Nate "knew" that the gun was now pointed directly toward his head and that Carmichael was a crack shot — even in semi-darkness — at this distance.

"I wouldn't do that if I were you, Babes." Nate spoke quietly, but he "knew" that the other had heard him. "You remember what happened to your two friends, don't you? And I wouldn't want to have to do that to you, too. I'd like to continue pretending that what we've meant to each other during the past three years wasn't all a sham."

However, the other continued to hold the gun aimed toward him.

"Put it down, Babes. Your mind is too easy to read — and to control! I can counter any command you give it. I've got powers you *can't even imagine*."

Nate heard a loud clatter behind him, and he "knew"

that Carmichael had dropped his weapon.

"One more thing, Babes... You might want to get on your little hotline to Washington and have a long talk with 'Cougar.' Maybe he might want to consider disbanding the whole agency; I think a little clique like yours that is even kept secret from the President may have outlived its usefulness, don't you? Oh...and, if I were you, I wouldn't get any ideas about coming after me in numbers, either. You see, numbers don't matter. I can be inside every one of their heads at the same time, manipulating them, and they won't even know I'm there."

Could he really do that? He didn't know. He couldn't know. He'd never been tested, and he might never know for certain until it was too late.

As he stepped over the rope at the bottom of the stairs with Sandy still squeezing his hand tightly, he heard a quiet moaning behind him.

EPILOGUE

Hours!

Maybe only minutes!

Nate sat, holding onto the hand of his unconscious mother.

It wasn't fair. She'd given him this "gift," but what could he offer her in return? Not a damn thing. He couldn't even postpone her death by as much as a second. What good was his super brain if he couldn't even help the ones he loved?

Slowly, he stood, wiped a tear away, and went over to stare out the window.

It was raining.

THE END

ABOUT THE AUTHOR

Neal Proud Deer has published millions of words over the course of his career as a staff writer, columnist, critic, and book author. He has also worked as a copy editor, news editor, managing editor, senior editor, and editor/publisher for several newspapers and magazines and has served on three college faculties.

More than 60 of his celebrity profiles have appeared on magazine covers, with interviews of such notables as President Jimmy Carter, poet Maya Angelou, actor Leonard Nimoy, baseball great Ozzie Smith, singers Peter, Paul & Mary, billionaire Steve Fossett, feminist and author Betty Friedan, television late-night host Jay Leno, comedian and social activist Bill Cosby, and Secretary of State Madeleine Albright.

His recent non-fiction book *Lights...Camera...Arch!* includes a foreword by award-winning film and television star John Goodman, and his book *Selling's Magic Words* was a major national seller in the 1980's and was utilized from coast to coast as a text by colleges and universities such as Purdue, California State, and the City University of New York.

His short fiction has appeared in print in various publications since the late 1960's. And his two sons are filmed screenwriters and staged playwrights living in Los Angeles.

Printed in the United States
137511LV00002B/5/P

9 781604 814125